THE BOBBSEY TWINS
OF LAKEPORT

The Bobbsey Twins
of Lakeport

By

LAURA LEE HOPE

GROSSET & DUNLAP
Publishers · New York

Published in 2004 by Grosset & Dunlap, a division of Penguin Young
Readers Group, 345 Hudson Street, New York, New York 10014.
GROSSET & DUNLAP is a trademark of Penguin Group (USA) Inc.
THE BOBBSEY TWINS® is a registered trademark of
Simon & Schuster, Inc.

Printed in the U.S.A.

ISBN 0-448-43752-X

3 5 7 9 10 8 6 4 2

CONTENTS

CHAPTER I

A MYSTERIOUS HOUSE

"ONE, two, three! Pull!"

There was a ripping sound as another plank of the tree house came loose. Bert and Freddie Bobbsey tossed it to the ground.

"Only one more," said six-year-old Freddie, tugging hard. He braced himself against the trunk of the tree which had been struck and split by lightning.

Waiting on the ground below were Bert's twin sister Nan, twelve, and blond Flossie, Freddie's twin. The girls were piling the lumber against the garage. Later a new house would be built in another tree.

"Watch it!" cried Bert suddenly, as Freddie slipped.

The little boy clutched wildly for a limb but missed it. He fell headfirst—into Nan's arms. The impact knocked them both to the ground.

Freddie skinned one knee. Nan banged her elbow.

"Oh, Freddie, you looked like a rocket coming down!" said Flossie, giggling. Then she became serious as her mother and father hurried to the children's side. "I know another house that's going to be knocked down," Flossie said. "That spooky old house by our school."

"Why do you say it's spooky?" Mrs. Bobbsey asked. She looked young and pretty standing beside her tall, athletic husband.

Freddie gave the answer. "Danny Rugg says it's haunted!"

"Really?" Bert asked from the tree. "You know Danny is always trying to scare you and Flossie. I wouldn't believe him."

Freddie did not answer. Instead, he said, "It will be fun to watch the house being torn down. They bring a great big ball on a crane and *wham*! They knock the walls down like this!" He cocked his fist and struck at the air with such force that he lost his balance and sat down hard on the grass.

As his older sister Nan helped him up she said teasingly, "That house really went down fast, Freddie!"

It was a Saturday morning in spring. The Bobbsey family was busy in the spacious yard which surrounded their rambling white house on a quiet street in Lakeport. The younger twins had helped clear the flower beds of fallen leaves while Mrs. Bobbsey and Nan were setting out new plants. Bert and his father had taken over the job of pruning the dead branches from the trees and bushes.

Now Mr. Bobbsey put down his long pruning shears. "You children must be talking about the old Marden house," he remarked. "When I was a boy that was a farm. But Lakeport has grown so much, the house is right in town!"

"Did the Mardens build the house, Dick?" Mrs. Bobbsey asked with interest.

"Yes. Old Mr. Marden had been ambassador to Great Britain, and when he retired he came to Lakeport. He bought several acres of land and put up that house. It was once a show place."

"Well, I think it's spooky now!" Flossie remarked with a little shudder.

"Why does Danny say that?" Nan asked curiously.

Danny Rugg was the same age as Bert and Nan. He was not popular with the other children because he was always playing mean tricks on them.

"Danny says that ghosts float in and out of those broken windows upstairs," Flossie reported, her eyes wide. "And he says if you go past there at night you can hear queer noises!"

Mr. Bobbsey rumpled Flossie's yellow curls. "Now, my little sweet fairy, you know there is no such thing as a ghost. The house is old and run down, but that's no reason to say it's spooky!"

Her father was fond of calling Flossie by this nickname. He had nicknamed Freddie his "little fireman" because Freddie liked to play with toy fire engines. Ever since he was a very small boy Freddie had said he was going to be a fireman when he grew up.

The discussion about the old house was interrupted when a jolly-looking woman stepped out onto the kitchen porch. She was Dinah Johnson, who helped Mrs. Bobbsey with the housework. Her husband Sam drove a truck at Mr. Bobbsey's lumberyard. Dinah and Sam lived in an apartment on the third floor of the Bobbsey house and were very popular with the whole family.

"How would you all like a picnic lunch?" Dinah called out.

"Oh, that would be fun!" Flossie exclaimed, running up to the porch. "May I help carry it out?"

Mrs. Bobbsey smiled as she pulled off her gardening gloves. "That's a splendid idea, Dinah. We can cook the hamburgers out here on the grill."

"I guess I'd better get my fire engine," Freddie said importantly. "We might have a fire, and you'd need me to put it out!"

He ran off and in a few minutes returned pulling a small red fire truck. It had a pumper attachment which squirted water.

In the meantime Bert brought a bag of charcoal from the garage. Soon he and his father had a fire going under the grill. Nan and Flossie covered the picnic table with a gay paper tablecloth, then set out paper plates, napkins, plastic forks, and cups.

"Will you cook the hamburgers, Dick?" Mrs. Bobbsey suggested.

Grinning, the twins' father slipped on the big white apron which Dinah held out and began to place the meat patties on the grill. Dinah went back to the kitchen and returned with a large bowl of potato salad. Nan and Flossie followed her, carrying a plate of buns and a relish dish of pickles and olives.

Now they joined the group clustered around the grill. "Umm, Daddy," Flossie cried, "they look bee-yoo-ti-ful!"

"Bring the platter, Nan," Mr. Bobbsey requested. "The burgers are ready."

Nan held out the large plate, and her father piled it high with delicious-looking, sizzling hamburgers.

"Now I'll put out the fire!" Freddie cried, running up with his toy engine. Lifting the small hose high he aimed it at the smoking grill.

But instead of reaching the charcoal, the stream of water went across the grill and hit

Flossie's bare knees! She squealed and turned to run. As she did, the little girl bumped into Nan. The plate of hamburgers teetered dangerously.

"Oh!" Nan exclaimed, trying to keep her balance and not spill everything. The hamburgers slid about on the platter but, miraculously, only one fell to the ground.

"Say, sis, you're quite a juggler!" Bert exclaimed when Nan finally set the platter on the table.

The others laughed and praised Nan for saving the food. Freddie giggled as he bit into his juicy sandwich and said, "These are good juggleburgers!"

When the last bit of lunch had been eaten, Mrs. Bobbsey spoke up. "This talk about the Marden house reminds me that I haven't been to see Mrs. Marden for a long time. I think I'll call on her this afternoon."

"Does she live in Lakeport?" Nan asked in surprise.

"Yes. She's an old lady now. Her husband was the grandson of the Mr. Marden who built the house. He died a few years ago. When the house was sold to the school last year, Mrs. Marden moved into a nursing home on the outskirts of town."

"Ask her if there's a ghost in her old house," Freddie spoke up.

His mother smiled. After she had left, the twins helped Dinah put away the picnic dishes. Then Bert said to the other children, "How about going over to take a look at the old house? Maybe we can find out what Danny's talking about!"

"Ooh! Do you think we should?" Flossie was still a little doubtful.

"Don't be a scaredycat, Flossie!" Freddie said. Flossie made a face at her twin, then ran down to the sidewalk. "All right," she called. "Come on!"

The others followed, and before long they were approaching the school. "Look!" Nan cried. "What are those men doing?"

In the open space between the school and the abandoned house, stood two young men. One was looking through a small telescope mounted on a tripod. The other held a pole and what looked like a long tape measure.

"I think they're surveyors," Bert replied. "Let's watch them work."

Noticing the children's curious expressions, one of the young men called out, "We're surveying for the addition to the school."

"This is our school," Flossie said as they reached the surveyors. Then glancing at the old Marden home, she asked, "Aren't you afraid of the haunted house?"

The young man shook his head and laughed. "Tim here," he said, nodding toward his companion, "has heard some strange sounds around the house, but I think they were just made by a couple of boys playing spook."

"We thought we'd go in and look around," Bert explained.

"I'm afraid you can't do that, sonny," the surveyor remarked. "The house is kept locked so vandals can't get in."

Seeing the children's disappointed faces, he laughed and added, "Keep your eyes open, and maybe the ghost will come out. Meanwhile, how would you like to help Tim and me?"

"Oh, yes!" Freddie and Flossie exclaimed in chorus. "That would be fun!"

Tim gave the small twins the pole to which the steel tape was attached and told them to walk toward the old house. "Then Joe will signal you which way to move."

Freddie and Flossie walked as far as the tape would permit. Then they turned to watch Joe who was peering through the telescope. "This is great," Freddie called. "I'm not going to be a fireman when I grow up. I'm going to be a surveyor!"

Joe waved his right hand, indicating the twins were to move the pole in that direction. Flossie fastened her eyes on the telescope. She did not see a little depression in the ground and stepped backward into it. Down she went, flat on her back!

In falling Flossie kept hold of the pole and by doing this pulled Freddie with her. Tim ran toward the tangle of legs, arms, pole, and metal tape. He helped both children to their feet.

"Are you hurt?" he asked anxiously.

Freddie and Flossie shook their heads. Then Freddie spoke up. "I don't think I'll be a surveyor after all," he announced with a grin.

Tim laughed. "Don't let one little fall discourage you," he advised. "You've been a big help to Joe and me."

Bert and Nan looked longingly at the old house. "I wish we could get in and look around," Bert said.

"I do too," Nan agreed. "I'd like to prove that there's nothing spooky about it!"

The twins discussed the old house as they walked toward their home. "Maybe Mother can tell us more about it," Flossie suggested.

When they reached home the children found Dinah in the kitchen getting ready to make cookies. "Your mother's not back yet," she told them, "and your father's gone downtown."

"What kind of cookies are you going to bake, Dinah?" Flossie asked.

"Chocolate walnut ones," the cook replied, "and if anybody around here wants to crack the nuts the cookies'll be done sooner!"

Flossie giggled. "I like to crack nuts. I'll help you!"

Nan volunteered to crack nuts too, and soon the girls were busy at the kitchen table, while Dinah bustled around mixing the batter in a large yellow bowl. Bert and Freddie wandered out to the yard.

Presently a car pulled into the drive, and in another minute Mrs. Bobbsey came in the back door followed by the boys.

"Mother says she has news for us," Bert said as Nan and Flossie looked up from their task.

"What is it?" Flossie asked, jumping up and throwing her arms about her mother.

Mrs. Bobbsey was silent for a moment as she looked around at the children's eager faces. Then she said smilingly, "I have a mystery for you to solve!"

CHAPTER II

THE OLD-FASHIONED KEY

"A MYSTERY?" Nan exclaimed. "Please, tell us what it is!"

"Yes, Mommy," Flossie echoed, hopping excitedly from one foot to the other. "What is it?"

The four children followed their mother into the living room and clustered about her as she sat down.

"Well," Mrs. Bobbsey began, "you remember I told you Mrs. Marden is a very old lady now and her memory is failing."

"That's too bad," said Flossie sympathetically. "Can't she remember *anything?*"

Mrs. Bobbsey smiled and hugged her small daughter. "Oh, yes, but she has difficulty recalling where she puts things. She told me jokingly that sometimes when she's looking for her glasses, she finds they are already on her nose!"

Flossie giggled, but Freddie put in impatiently, "But what's the mystery, Mother?"

13

"Well, it seems that some very valuable souvenirs which Mrs. Marden treasured have disappeared!"

"What are they?"

"Where are they?"

"Do they have anything to do with the ghost?"

The questions came thick and fast. Mrs. Bobbsey held up her hands. "If you'll listen, I'll tell you all about it," she promised with a smile.

When the children were quiet again, their mother went on with her story. "You recall Daddy told you that the Mr. Marden who built the house next to the school had been ambassador to Great Britain?"

The twins nodded eagerly.

"Well, when Mr. Marden left England he was presented with two very valuable tokens by the royal family. One was a beautiful cameo brooch surrounded by diamonds."

"What's a cameo?" Flossie asked.

"A cameo," Mrs. Bobbsey explained, "is made by carving a shell or precious stone which has layers of different colors. It is carved so that a figure of one color stands out against a background of another color."

"That sounds pretty," Nan commented.

"The other thing Mrs. Marden misplaced," said Mrs. Bobbsey, "was a collection of rare obsidional coins."

"What are obsid'nal coins?" Freddie wanted to know. "A special kind of money?"

"Money?" Mrs. Bobbsey smiled. "I think it would be a good idea for Bert to look up obsidional coins in our book on coins. Mrs. Marden wasn't very clear about them, but she is sure they are rare and valuable."

At this moment Mr. Bobbsey came into the room and was told the story of the missing articles. "I'd like to know what those coins are too," he remarked. "Get the book, Bert."

Bert went to the bookshelves and returned with a thick volume. He leafed through the pages. "Here they are," he cried. "They're also called siege coins or coins of necessity. They were made in Europe by cities and towns under siege to pay off the defending troops."

"How old are they, Bert?" Mr. Bobbsey asked.

"Here are some pictures of coins from the sixteenth and seventeenth centuries." Bert held out the book so the others could see the illustrations.

"Why, the coins are four-sided!" Nan cried in astonishment.

"Yes," Bert agreed as he read on. "They were made from any material the authorities could find—melted-down statues and church silver. Often they were irregularly shaped."

"I'd love to see some coins like that," Nan said

eagerly. "Where did Mrs. Marden keep them? And when did they disappear?"

Mrs. Bobbsey looked distressed. "Mrs. Marden said she put them away in a very safe place in the old house, but she hasn't been able to remember where!"

"Oh Mother, how dreadful!" Nan exclaimed. "What can she do?"

Mrs. Bobbsey smiled. "I told Mrs. Marden you twins enjoy solving mysteries, and she said—"

"What?" they asked eagerly.

"That perhaps you would hunt for the lost gifts for her!"

"Great!" Bert cried out. "It sounds like a real mystery!"

"Do you mean we'd have to go into that spooky house?" Flossie asked, shivering a little.

"How can we?" Nan queried. "The surveyors said it was locked!"

Mr. Bobbsey spoke up. "I should think your school principal, Mr. Tetlow, would give you permission to go in if you explained the situation," he suggested.

Gray-haired Mr. Tetlow, although strict in discipline, was well liked by most of the children. The four twins were very fond of him.

"Sure, Dad!" Bert agreed. "I'll bet he would!"

"Let's find out on Monday," Nan proposed.

"Mother," said Flossie, "did you ask Mrs. Marden about the ghost?"

"She just laughed at such an idea," Mrs. Bobbsey answered.

It seemed to the twins that Monday would never come, they were so eager to begin their search. But Monday finally did arrive and after a good breakfast of Dinah's special pancakes, the children started off to school.

On the way they met a boy and a girl who were Bert's and Nan's best friends. Charlie Mason was about Bert's height and like Bert he had dark hair and brown eyes. Nellie Parks, Nan's chum, was a pretty blond girl with blue eyes.

"Hi, twins!" Nellie called as the six children reached the corner at the same time.

"Hello, Nellie!" Flossie replied. "We're going to solve a mystery!"

"You are?" Nellie asked, her blue eyes widening with interest. "What's the mystery about?"

Bert and Nan took turns telling their friends the story of Mrs. Marden and the valuable cameo and coins which she had misplaced.

"Whew!" Charlie exclaimed. "That *is* a mystery! Are you going to search the old house?"

"Yes," Bert replied. "Would you and Nellie like to help us?"

"I sure would," Charlie said. "How about you, Nellie?"

Nellie eagerly agreed, and the children discussed the old house the rest of the way to school. As they walked into the building Charlie asked, "When are you planning to talk to Mr. Tetlow?"

"Nan and I are going to his office right after school this afternoon," Bert replied.

"Okay," Charlie said. "Nellie and I will meet you in the hall and hear the result."

"Keep your fingers crossed," Bert said with a grin.

The day seemed very long. From where Nan sat in her homeroom she could see the deserted Marden house. It was a large three-story building which at one time had been painted white. Now the paint was worn and chipped. The once green shutters hung at crazy angles. Two of the windows in the second story had been broken, and at one of them Nan could see a torn window shade waving to and fro.

"Where could Mrs. Marden have hidden the cameo and coins?" Nan mused. "If she just left them in a cupboard or closet, perhaps someone has already found them and taken them away. Wouldn't it be sad if Mrs. Marden never got her things back?"

Finally the afternoon classes drew to a close. Nan and Bert walked to the principal's office which was located on the first floor and went in.

"Is Mr. Tetlow expecting you?" the school secretary inquired.

Nan spoke up. "No, but Bert and I have a question we'd like to ask him if he isn't too busy."

The young woman went into the principal's private office and returned in a few minutes. "Mr. Tetlow says to come in," she announced with a smile.

Mr. Tetlow greeted them from behind his large desk. "I'm glad to see you, Nan and Bert," he said. "I hope you're not in any trouble."

"Oh, no," Nan replied. "We just want your help in solving a mystery."

The principal leaned back in his chair and took off his glasses. "Well now, that sounds very interesting," he said. "What kind of a mystery is it?"

Quickly Bert explained about Mrs. Marden and the fact that she could not remember where she had hidden the valuable souvenirs. "We thought that if we could search the old house before it's torn down we might find them for her," he ended.

"And the surveyors told us the house was locked," Nan said. "We hoped you might unlock it for us."

Mr. Tetlow explained that although all the furniture had been taken out of the house, the school authorities had decided it should be kept locked so that no prowlers could get in.

"Sometimes old houses are ransacked of good wood, plumbing fixtures, and lighting fixtures which can be sold," Mr. Tetlow went on. "But I see no objection to your looking through the house for Mrs. Marden's property. You're responsible children, so I'll let you take our extra key for a few days. Just be sure to bring it to school each day in case anyone needs to get into the house. I have a key, but I might not be available at the moment."

Nan's eyes were shining. "Thank you, Mr. Tetlow," she said. "We'll be very careful and lock the house each time."

The principal opened a drawer of his desk and took out a large, old-fashioned key. "This is it," he said. "Perhaps we'd better mark it," he added with a twinkle in his eyes, "so if you should happen to lose the key, the finder could send it back."

As Nan and Bert watched, Mr. Tetlow took up a white tag and tied it to the key. Then in tiny letters he wrote on the tag: "Marden house, property of Lakeport School Board." Then he handed it to Bert.

"Thank you, sir," Bert said. "I'll be very careful not to lose the key," he added.

"I know you will," Mr. Tetlow said with a smile. "Good luck with your mystery solving, Nan and Bert. I hope you find Mrs. Marden's valuables for her."

When the twins left the principal's office they found Charlie and Nellie waiting in the hall.

"What did he say?" Nellie asked eagerly. "May we go in the house?"

In reply Bert pulled the big key from his pocket and dangled it in front of Nellie. "What do you think this is?" he asked teasingly.

"Say, that's great!" Charlie exclaimed. "Let's get on with the Marden mystery!"

As the four children started toward the school entrance, a boy stepped from the classroom near where they had been standing. He was taller and heavier than Bert and Charlie and had an unpleasant expression on his face.

"Danny Rugg!" Nellie exclaimed. "Have you been spying on us?"

"Why should I spy on you silly kids?" Danny replied scornfully. "But you'd better keep out of that old house. It's haunted! I know!"

CHAPTER III

THE SEARCH BEGINS

BERT and Nan looked at each other. "What makes you so sure the house is haunted?" Nan asked Danny scornfully.

Danny shrugged and walked away. "Just don't say I didn't warn you!" he called back over his shoulder.

"Don't pay any attention to him!" Charlie advised. "You know he's always trying to make trouble."

"He's doing his best to scare us so we won't find Mrs. Marden's things," Nan declared heatedly.

"That's right, Sis," Bert agreed. "Let's go in the house and look around."

Followed by the other three, Bert walked over to the deserted old mansion. As he put the key in the lock there came a giggle and Freddie and Flossie stuck their heads from around the corner of the porch.

"We waited for you," Freddie announced. "Flossie and I want to go inside the haunted house too!"

"All right, come along," Nan said as Bert turned the key and opened the door into a wide center hall.

The six children walked in and looked around. At one side of the hall they could see a stairway. The broad steps were littered with bits of fallen plaster. The scenic paper which covered the walls was stained and peeling in places.

"Ooh, it *is* sort of spooky!" Nellie remarked with a little shiver.

There were four closed doors, two on each side of the hall. Gingerly the children opened the one on the left. It led into the living room. There was a large fireplace at the far end.

The playmates crossed the hall and opened the other door. "This must have been the dining room," Nan said, seeing built-in cupboards in two corners of the room.

"And this was the library," Bert guessed as they went into the room behind the living room. Two walls were covered by bookshelves which extended almost to the ceiling.

The fourth door proved to lead to a small corridor at the far end of which was the kitchen.

"What a 'normous cooking fireplace!" Flossie exclaimed. The big opening took up almost the entire end of the room. It was blocked now with logs piled high.

"In olden days people did their cooking in fireplaces," Nan said.

"Let's see what's upstairs," Bert proposed.

There was a narrow flight of stairs leading from the kitchen, and the children crept up them carefully. On the second floor they found five more rooms. Here again paper was hanging from the walls in strips. Closet doors stood open, and torn window shades hung at crazy angles over the windows.

"It doesn't look as if there are very many places to search," Nan said in discouragement. "Everything seems to have been cleared out!"

"We could break up into teams," Bert suggested, "and look through the rooms very carefully."

At that moment the children heard a loud *bang!* Flossie screamed. "It's the ghost!" she cried.

"What *was* that?" Nellie asked, her voice shaking a little.

Bert walked over to a window and peered out. "I think that's the ghost," he said with a grin.

The others gathered behind him, and he pointed to a loose shutter. As they watched, a gust of wind struck the shutter and banged it against the side of the house.

"Just the same," Flossie quavered, "I want to go home!"

"All right, honey," Nan replied. "It's getting late anyway. We'll come back some other time."

At breakfast the next morning Flossie said, "Mother, I want to see Mrs. Marden and ask her about the things she hid. Maybe by now she remembers where they are."

"All right, dear. I'm going out that way this afternoon. I could drop you and Nan off at the nursing home if you like."

Bert looked up from his bacon and eggs. "This would be a good day for you to go. I have baseball practice after school, so we couldn't search the old house anyway."

It was agreed that Mrs. Bobbsey would pick up Nan and Flossie at the end of the school day. As soon as the dismissal bell rang that afternoon the girls took their coats from the locker room and dashed outside. Mrs. Bobbsey was waiting for them.

"Oh, I do hope Mrs. Marden has remembered where she put her things," Flossie said as she climbed into the car.

"I hope so, too," Mrs. Bobbsey remarked. "But you know, dear, Mrs. Marden is a very old lady and when one gets to be her age, one is apt to be forgetful."

A short time later the car drew up before the

comfortable-looking nursing home. Mrs. Bobb-sey handed Nan a box. "Here are some cookies Dinah baked for Mrs. Marden. I'll be back in about an hour to pick you girls up," she said.

Flossie and Nan waved good-by to their mother as they ran up the stone walk to the front door. A nurse brought Mrs. Marden to the reception room and Nan introduced herself and Flossie.

"It's very nice of you to come to see me," the elderly woman said, giving each girl a little hug.

"Dinah sent you some cookies," Nan said and gave Mrs. Marden the package.

"Thank you, dear," the elderly woman replied. "We have tea here each afternoon. Would you like to pass the cookies around to my friends at that time? It's my turn to pour the tea today."

Flossie could wait no longer to ask a question of her own. "Have you remembered where you hid the pin and the coins?" she asked breathlessly.

Mrs. Marden shook her head and told the girls that although she had tried very hard she could not recall the hiding place of the valuable gifts. At that moment several more elderly women came into the room, and Mrs. Marden introduced Nan and Flossie to them. A maid rolled in a tea cart.

Mrs. Marden sat down and began to pour the

tea. "Would you girls like cambric tea?" she asked with a smile.

"What is that?" Nan asked curiously.

Mrs. Marden filled a cup almost full of milk, then added a little tea and sugar and handed it to Nan. She then fixed a similar cup for Flossie.

"It's good!" Flossie exclaimed. Nan agreed.

When the tea had been poured Flossie passed a plate of Dinah's cookies, then sat down next to Mrs. Marden.

"Can't you sing us a little song?" the old lady asked her.

Flossie looked hesitant, but Nan encouraged

her with a smile. "I have one I made up myself," she said finally, "and I dance to it."

When the ladies said they thought this would be very nice, Flossie stood up. As she danced around the room she sang a little song about a cricket. It ended, "And the cricket on your hearth goes chirp, chirp, chirp!"

As the other women applauded, Mrs. Marden looked excited. "That's it!" she exclaimed. "The hearth! It has something to do with my lost treasure!"

"Oh, can you think of anything more?" Nan asked breathlessly.

The elderly woman's expression grew sad. "No. I thought I had it for a moment, but it's gone now!"

"Never mind," Flossie said consolingly. "We'll find the things for you!"

In a few minutes Mrs. Bobbsey came for the girls, and they said good-by to the guests of the nursing home. "Do come again," Mrs. Marden called as they got into the car.

That evening at the supper table Nan and Flossie described their visit to the nursing home. When they told how excited the elderly woman had been at the mention of a hearth, Bert snapped his fingers.

"Maybe the treasure is hidden under the hearth of one of the fireplaces in the house!

There may be a stone which lifts out!" he reasoned.

"There are lots of fireplaces in that house," Freddie recalled.

"Let's search tomorrow after school," Nan suggested, and the others agreed.

But when the next day came Freddie and Flossie decided to go home with some of their little friends to play after school. Nan met Bert in the hall.

"Nellie and I have to go to a meeting," she explained. "I'll meet you later at the Marden house."

There was to be a new gymnasium in the addition to the school, and the children were organizing different activities to raise money for modern equipment. Nan and Nellie were members of one of the committees.

"Okay," Bert agreed. "I'll hang around until you're free."

Bert wandered out into the schoolyard Charlie Mason came running up.

"Are you going to search the old house again?" he asked eagerly. "I have to go home now. My mother made a dentist appointment for me. I can help look tomorrow, though," he added.

Bert said he was waiting for Nan and they would probably go to the house. "I'll let you know if we find anything," he promised Charlie.

"If we don't, we'll all look again tomorrow."

As Charlie ran off, a couple of other boys hailed Bert. "Come on and play ball," Ralph Blake called. "We need one more for our side."

"I'm waiting for my sister," Bert answered, "but I'll play until she comes."

Danny Rugg had joined the group of ball players. When he heard Bert's reply, he snickered. "Bertie Boy would rather play with girls," he taunted him.

Bert Bobbsey clenched his fists and walked toward the bully. "Are you looking for a fight, Danny?" he asked.

Danny backed away. "Come on, let's play ball if we're going to," he protested.

The other boys came up and the game began. In a short while the score stood five to six with Bert's team ahead. When Danny came to bat there was a man on base. This was his team's chance to win the game!

"Come on, Danny!" called Jack Barton on Danny's team. "Let's have a home run!"

The pitch came toward Danny. He swung and gave the ball a terrific wallop. Danny raced around the bases as Bert ran back. The next second Bert had caught the ball! The game was over and Bert's side had won!

Danny's face was red with rage. "You think you're so smart, Bert Bobbsey," he yelled, "let me see you catch this one!" He picked up a ball and threw it viciously at Bert who was walking toward the school building.

"Duck!" cried Ned Brown.

As Bert stooped, the fast ball sped over his head. *Crash!* It smashed through a window!

CHAPTER IV

THE SECRET TRAP DOOR

WHEN Danny saw the ball hit the school window he turned pale. The next minute he ran from the yard as fast as he could! A moment later Mr. Tetlow appeared at the door of the building.

"Who threw that ball?" he asked sternly.

The boys shuffled their feet and were silent. Mr. Tetlow's expression softened. "I suppose you don't want to tell on a schoolmate," he said. "However, I have a good idea who is to blame."

The principal went back into the school as Bert and the others heaved sighs of relief. The ball players with the exception of Bert trickled off toward their homes. In a few minutes Nan ran up to her twin.

"Nellie couldn't stay either," she announced, "so you and I are the only ones left to search."

As the two children walked toward the old

house, Bert told his sister about the broken window.

"That was just like Danny to run away!" she said indignantly. "I'm surprised he didn't try to put the blame on you!"

Bert grinned. "In a way it was my fault. If I hadn't ducked, Danny would have hit me instead of the window!"

"It's a good thing he didn't," Nan replied. "He might have hurt you badly!"

Bert took the old-fashioned iron key from his pocket and unlocked the front door of the deserted house. "Shall we divide up the rooms to save time?" he asked as he and Nan stepped into the dim hall.

Nan nodded. "I'll take the left side of the first floor and you take the right. If we don't find anything, then we can go upstairs together."

Bert walked into the old living room and over to the fireplace. The hearth and the space surrounding the opening were fashioned of blue and white tiles. On each one was a picture of some animal or a flower.

"I wonder if one is loose," Bert murmured. He knelt down and carefully ran his fingers over each tile on the hearth. Several were cracked, but all of them seemed to fit solidly together and he could move nothing.

Next Bert examined the tiles on each side of the fireplace. He took a knife from his pocket and tapped them, listening for any sound which might tell him one was loose. Again he had no success.

He peered up the inside of the fireplace, but there was only a small flue and no place for anything to be hidden. Next Bert walked slowly around the room, paying special attention to the baseboard and window frames. There seemed to be no hiding place there.

"Well, I'll try the library," he told himself. Here again he examined the hearth carefully. This one was made of bricks, but they too seemed to be set solidly and did not move when Bert pressed them.

"There's certainly nothing hidden in either of these hearths," he murmured. "I'll take a look at the bookshelves."

He searched all the shelves within reach. Then, standing against the opposite wall on tiptoe, he gazed at the upper shelves. There was nothing to be seen.

Suddenly Bert heard Nan scream! He ran.

Earlier, when Nan had entered the dining room, she had gone immediately to the old fireplace. This one was paneled in wood. Carefully she had tapped each panel and tried to move it, but without success.

Next she moved to the corner cupboards and felt the wooden backs and sides. "I don't believe there's anything hidden in this room," she finally

The trap door was slowly closing!

decided. "Maybe I'll have better luck in the kitchen."

Nan had walked quietly down the hall and turned into the small passageway leading to the kitchen. She opened the door and stood rooted to the floor. A trap door in front of the huge fireplace was slowly closing! As it fell into place she screamed!

Bert dashed into the room. "What's the matter, Sis?" he asked anxiously.

Nan pointed to the floor. "Th-there's a trapdoor right there, and somebody just went through it!" she cried.

Her brother ran to the spot. "You're right, Nan!" he exclaimed. "I can see the outlines, but there's no way to open it from this side!"

"Wh-who do you suppose it was?" Nan was still trembling.

"It's probably Danny Rugg trying to scare us," Bert assured her. "You remember he warned us about coming in the house."

"I suppose it was Danny," Nan said, reassured by Bert's reply. "Wait until I see him in the morning!"

"I think we'd annoy him more if we pretended not to know he'd been here," Bert suggested.

"All right." Nan giggled. "And let's not say anything about it to Freddie and Flossie. They might worry."

So when Bert and Nan got home they said nothing about the trap door to the younger twins but reported only that they had not found the missing gifts. Nan changed the subject by telling her mother and Dinah about the money-making project which had been discussed at school that afternoon.

"We girls are going to sell cookies on Saturdays," she announced. "Will you help me make some, Dinah?"

Dinah beamed. "I sure will, honey! You just tell me what kind you want!"

"That sounds like a very good idea, Nan," Mrs. Bobbsey said. "We'll all help you."

"Thanks, Mother and Dinah," Nan said happily. "We'll probably start this Saturday."

Although Bert said nothing at home about the incident of the broken window, he was still worried about it the next day. Then at recess Danny walked up to him, a frown on his face.

"You're a fine tattletale!" the bully said angrily.

"What do you mean?"

"You know what I mean! You told old Tetlow that I threw the ball that smashed that window."

"I didn't say anything of the sort!" Bert defended himself.

"He called me in the office as soon as I got

here this morning," Danny said, "and told me I'd have to pay for a new window! How would he know I broke it unless you told him?"

"He probably saw you! Anyway you were the only one who ran away!" Bert replied.

"I still think you tattled," Danny said sullenly.

Bert was so angry at Danny's persistence that he forgot his resolution to say nothing about the trap door. "You needn't think you scared Nan and me in the old house either!" he blurted out.

"What are you talking about?" Danny asked scornfully. "I haven't tried to scare you!"

"Come on, Danny!" Bert protested. "You know you were in the house and went down through that trap door in the kitchen yesterday afternoon!"

Danny shook his head. "You're really crazy, Bert! I don't know anything about a trap door." Then he grinned slyly. "But remember, I told you the house was haunted. Maybe you saw the ghost in the kitchen!"

"You're the one who's crazy!" Bert cried. "You know there's no such thing as a ghost!"

"Oh no?" Danny walked away, whistling.

Bert continued to puzzle over the episode of the trap door the rest of the day. He was reluctantly convinced that Danny had not been in the house. But who could have been? The place was supposed to be locked and anyone who had a right to be in the house would not have run away when Nan came into the kitchen.

"Did Mr. Tetlow find out that Danny broke the window?" Nan whispered as she and Bert were leaving their homeroom at the end of the day.

"Yes, and he thinks I told on him," Bert replied. "But he insists he wasn't in the Marden house later."

"Oh, Bert! We weren't going to say anything about that!" Nan protested.

"I know," Bert said sheepishly, "but I got so mad at him that I forgot!"

They had reached the outside door by this time and noticed a group of children standing near by. They seemed to be watching something on the ground.

Bert pushed forward. "What's going on, Charlie?" he asked his chum, who stood at the edge of the group.

"They're pouring concrete for the new driveway," Charlie replied. "Come on and watch them."

Charlie, Bert, and Nan walked around to the other side of the driveway where the concrete mixer stood. The earthen bed had been prepared and marked off by narrow wooden frames.

Two men worked with long wooden rakes to spread the liquid cement within the framework.

The children watched with interest.

"That would be fun to do," Bert observed and Charlie nodded.

The concrete mixer made so much noise that it was difficult to hear anything else.

"How long does it take the concrete to harden?" Charlie wondered.

"I don't know exactly, but if you step in it when it's wet, your print stays there forever."

All this time Freddie and Flossie had been staying late in their class. The teacher, Miss Earle, was reading a story aloud. When the dismissal bell rang, she looked up. "Shall I finish the story tomorrow?" she asked.

"Oh no," the children chorused. "Please finish it now!"

Miss Earle smiled and continued reading. In a few minutes she closed the book. "That is the end," she announced. "Did you like the story?" she asked.

"Yes, Miss Earle!" they cried.

When Freddie and Flossie had put on their coats they met in the hall. Freddie ran up and tapped his twin on the arm. "You're it!" he cried and raced down the hall.

Most of the children had left the school by this time and the hall was empty. Flossie ran after Freddie and tagged him. "Now you're it!" she teased, dashing away.

With a grin Freddie stepped into an empty

classroom. When Flossie turned around to see if her twin was catching up to her, he was nowhere in sight.

"He's trying to play a trick on me," Flossie told herself and began to tiptoe back down the long hall.

When she reached the empty classroom Freddie jumped out at her. Flossie screamed, then ran toward the outside door, crying, "You can't catch me!"

Outside the building Bert had turned to reply to Charlie's question about the concrete when he looked up and saw Flossie run out the front door. She was looking back and did not notice what was being done to the driveway. Bert opened his mouth to call to her, but it was too late.

Flossie ran right into the soft cement!

CHAPTER V

FREDDIE'S ADVENTURE

AS HER little feet sank into the gooey mass, Flossie gave a shriek. "Help!" she cried. "I'm stuck!"

"Stand still!" Nan called to her.

But Flossie was too excited to hear her sister. She tried to take a step. Her feet came out of her shoes which remained stuck tight in the cement. Now she was caught again, this time in her socks.

"Wait a minute, Flossie!" Bert cried. "We'll get you loose."

"Here are some boards," Charlie called. He ran over to a pile of laths and came back with several of the thin strips of wood.

Bert and Charlie laid them together across the driveway near Flossie. The little girl, slipping out of her socks, stepped from the wet cement onto the wood. Carefully she made her way to safety. When Flossie reached solid ground, Bert crawled onto the makeshift bridge and pulled out Flossie's shoes and socks.

"Your footprints will be there forever," Nellie remarked.

"Ooh, I'm so sorry," Flossie apologized to the workman who was laying the pavement. "I didn't know it was soft!"

The man patted her yellow curls. "That's all right," he said. "I believe I can smooth the cement over. Unless," he added teasingly, "you want your footprints to stay here!"

Flossie shook her head vigorously. "No, please cover them up," she said.

At that moment Mrs. Parks drove up to take Nellie home. When she saw Flossie's bare feet she asked in surprise what had happened.

Flossie looked embarrassed and explained.

"Gracious!" Mrs. Parks exclaimed. "Hop in the car and I'll take you all home."

When they reached the Bobbsey house Bert picked Flossie up and carried her inside. He set her down in the kitchen, saying, "I'll get this cement off your shoes before it hardens, but I'm afraid your socks are ruined!"

Mrs. Bobbsey laughed when she heard the story of Flossie's accident. "I was planning to get you some new shoes anyway," she said, "so we'll go downtown tomorrow afternoon. I'll pick you and Freddie up at school."

Flossie loved to go shopping with her mother and eagerly agreed. Freddie was not so sure.

"Oh, come on, Freddie," his twin pleaded. "We'll ride the escater."

Seeing Mrs. Bobbsey's puzzled look, Nan laughed. "I think she means the escalator, Mother."

"That's what I said," Flossie insisted. "The stairs that go up and down by themselves."

Remembering the escalator from previous trips, Freddie decided it would be fun after all to go shopping.

The next afternoon when he and Flossie and Mrs. Bobbsey reached Taylor's large department store, the small twins were overwhelmed by the window display. "Oh, Mother," Flossie begged, "let's look in the windows first!"

In one was a large arrangement of dolls. They were of all sizes and kinds. One corner of the window was enclosed by a little white picket fence, and inside the fence was a toy barn. Dolls dressed as farmers and country girls were shown pitching hay, milking cows, and feeding tiny chickens.

"Isn't it just bee-yoo-ti-ful?" Flossie exclaimed in delight.

"I like this side better," Freddie said, pointing to a little airplane hangar. Toy planes were zooming through the air, and on the ground were tiny soldiers in Air Force uniforms.

Mrs. Bobbsey finally persuaded the twins to go into the store. "The shoe department is on the third floor, and if you like we'll go up on the escalator," she said.

It was fun standing on the steps and watching the first floor drop away beneath them. They had reached the second floor before they realized it.

"Be careful getting off," Mrs. Bobbsey cautioned.

Freddie and Flossie both watched until the step on which they were standing was even with the floor and then hopped off quickly.

"I love escaters," Flossie observed as she stepped onto the next series of moving stairs.

When they arrived at the third floor, Mrs. Bobbsey led the way to the shoe department. A pleasant salesman waited on them, and Flossie was soon fitted with a shiny new pair of shoes.

"I'm going back to the housewares department," Mrs. Bobbsey said. "Dinah wants a new kind of cake pan. You children may look around on this floor until I'm through."

Mrs. Bobbsey walked off, and Flossie and Freddie began to stroll through the various departments. Flossie saw a counter of special dolls and doll clothes and ran over to examine them.

"My dollies really need some new spring clothes," she said to herself as she looked at the tempting display. There were dresses and shorts and bathing suits. And even little coats made of fur. On another counter she admired tiny brush and comb sets and mirrors with pink and blue backs.

Freddie was not interested in doll clothes. He stopped a minute to watch a salesman demonstrating a toy airplane, then wandered on. He found himself back at the escalator. Many people were riding up on it, but he saw no way of going down.

"I guess you have to walk down the stairs," he told himself. "I think I'll go down and ride up again while Flossie is looking at those dolls. She won't miss me."

Freddie looked around and noticed a door marked "Stairway." He quickly ran down two flights of stairs and then another. When he reached the bottom he found himself in the basement of the store.

Here was the department which sold mechanical toys. Freddie saw a little train going round and round on a track. Bells were ringing and signals flashing.

"That's keen!" he thought. "I wonder how it works."

He walked over to the display and watched it in fascination. Then he moved on to a section where there were small model automobiles. A salesman hailed him. "How about a ride, sonny?"

Freddie's eyes grew large. "May I really drive one?" he asked breathlessly.

"Sure!" The salesman showed him how to operate the little vehicle, and soon Freddie was riding around the cleared floor space, a happy smile on his face. When he climbed out of the little car he noticed a group of toy fire engines so he walked over to look at them.

By this time Freddie had covered almost the entire basement floor of the large store. He decided it was time to go back upstairs where his mother and Flossie were waiting.

"Let's see," he said to himself, "I think the moving stairs were over this way." But although Freddie thought he walked in the right direction, he was hopelessly mixed up. The little boy could not find either the stairway or the escalator.

He went through a doorway and found himself in another part of the basement. It seemed to be a storage room. At one end a man sat at a desk checking off items in a large ledger.

Freddie started toward him. "Please, can you tell me how I get up to the third floor?" the little boy asked.

But the busy man evidently did not hear Freddie because he closed the book and walked through a doorway back of him. Freddie ran after the man, pulling the door shut behind him. He was just in time to see the man go through a wide doorway. As he did an overhead door slid down and Freddie heard a catch fall into place.

The little boy looked around. He was in a large room lined with paper cartons and wooden boxes. In one corner was a big pile of excelsior.

"I think I'll sit down on that soft stuff for a moment," Freddie thought with a sigh. He was tired, and the room was very warm.

In a few minutes Freddie's eyes closed and his head fell forward. He was soon fast asleep!

In the meantime, back at school Bert and Charlie were waiting for Nan and Nellie to come outside. Bert had told his friend about the trap door in the kitchen of the old Marden house.

"Nan and I can't figure out how anyone got into the house to open it," Bert said.

Charlie smiled. "I wouldn't trust Danny Rugg even if he did say he wasn't in there. Maybe he followed you and Nan when you weren't looking and sneaked down cellar."

At this moment Nan and Nellie came out of the school building. "I'm so excited," Nellie exclaimed. "I can't wait to look through that house again. Maybe today we'll find the lost treasure!"

Since Bert and Nan had thoroughly explored the first floor, the four children ascended the stairs to the rooms on the second. Each one took a bedroom and searched it carefully. They followed the same procedure which Bert and Nan had used two days earlier, paying particular attention to the fireplaces. But they found nothing.

Nellie finished her room first and went into the fifth bedroom. Suddenly she called to the others, "Come in here! I think I see something on the closet shelf!"

Nan, Bert, and Charlie ran to her side. By standing on their tiptoes and craning their necks they could see what looked like a package in the far corner of the closet shelf.

"Nan, you're the lightest," Bert said. "I'll boost you up so you can reach it."

Bert bent over, and Nan climbed onto his back. She stretched her arm and just managed to work the package forward with the tips of her fingers. It fell to the floor with a little thud!

"Oh, I just know it's the cameo and coins!" Nellie cried excitedly.

Her hands shaking in anticipation, Nan undid the brown paper package. When they saw the contents, the children groaned in disappointment. Spread on the paper were four old-fashioned casters for chair legs!

"I was sure I had found the treasure!" Nellie said mournfully as she wrapped the casters up again and replaced them on the closet shelf.

"There's still the attic to search," Nan said, trying to sound cheerful.

"Sure!" Charlie agreed. "Don't be downhearted!"

The stairs leading to the attic were narrow, rickety, and winding. The four crept up them carefully. When they reached the top, the children looked around. A window at each end of the long room let in a small amount of light.

The place had evidently been cleared out some time before. The floor was covered with dust, and the only article in the whole space was an old-fashioned trunk under one of the eaves.

"There's not much here to search," Bert observed. "But let's have a look at that trunk!"

It was dark under the eaves so the two boys dragged the old chest into the middle of the room. The catch was rusty, but Charlie managed to pry it open. He pulled up the lid.

The tray in the top was empty except for a few stray buttons. Eagerly Bert lifted out the tray to disclose the inside of the trunk. There were layers of old-fashioned dresses which gave off a musty odor.

Nan ran her hand around the edges of the trunk. "There's no box here," she said. "But it might be fun to look at the dresses."

"It's getting dark," Nellie remarked. "Maybe we'd better wait and examine the dresses some other time."

The others agreed. "We can all think about the lost treasures over the week end and perhaps someone will have a brilliant idea where to look next," Bert added cheerfully.

"We'll come back Monday," Nan agreed. "We just *have* to find those things for Mrs. Marden!"

She led the way down the narrow stairs. Nan had almost reached the bottom when she turned to say something to Nellie, who was behind her.

The next second Nan pitched headfirst onto the floor! She lay very still.

CHAPTER VI

THE PROWLER

"NAN!" Nellie screamed, jumping down the last few steps and bending over her friend.

Bert and Charlie quickly joined her. "The bottom step is missing!" Bert exclaimed. "That's what made her fall!"

His twin lay pale and quiet. "She's knocked out!" Nellie said. "I'll run across to the school and get some water!" She was off in a flash.

In a few minutes she was back, a cup of water in her hand. By this time Nan was sitting up, but she was still groggy from her fall.

"Thank you, Nellie," she said faintly as she took a sip of water. "I feel all right now."

Bert and Charlie each took one of her arms and helped her down the stairs to the front door. As they reached the yard, Danny Rugg came dashing up.

"What's going on?" he wanted to know. "I saw

Nellie running in here with a cup in her hand!"

"As if you didn't know!" Bert said angrily. "You sneaked in here behind us and took that step out so one of us would fall!"

Bert dropped Nan's arm and walked down to where Danny stood. "You're trying to get even with me because you think I squealed on you when you broke the window. Well, I didn't!"

"I don't know anything about any old step," Danny replied. "Get out of my way!" With that, he gave Bert a hard shove which made the boy almost lose his balance.

This was too much for Bert. He doubled up his fist and punched Danny on the shoulder. Danny hit back, striking Bert on the side of the face. In another minute the two were rolling on the ground, each trying to land a blow on the other.

At this point Mr. Tetlow ran out of the school building. "Bert and Danny!" he called. "Stop that fighting at once!"

The boys struggled to their feet, still glaring at each other.

"Now tell me what this is all about!" Mr. Tetlow commanded sternly. "You begin, Bert!"

"Nan just had a bad fall in the Marden house because someone took out a step while we were in the attic," Bert explained. "I think Danny did it!"

"I don't know anything about it," Danny

whined. "I was just standing here, and Bert hit me!"

"What makes you think Danny played such a trick, Bert?" Mr. Tetlow asked.

"Well, I—"

As Bert started to explain, they all heard the back door of the old house close with a bang. Then they were startled to see a man's figure dash across the narrow back yard and disappear through a hedge!

"It seems that there was somebody else in the house, Bert," the principal observed. "Perhaps you should apologize to Danny for accusing him!"

Bert hung his head. "I'm sorry, Danny. I guess I did make a mistake," he said.

"Okay," Danny replied gruffly as he walked away, "but don't always be blaming me for everything!"

"Come into my office, Bert and Nan," Mr. Tetlow requested. "I want to hear about what happened in the house."

After Bert and Nan had told him about the missing step and also about the trap door, the principal reached for the telephone on his desk.

"All right, children. I won't keep you any longer, but I'm going to report this whole business to the police and the fact that there was a prowler in the house. If you see anything else suspicious, come and tell me at once."

Charlie and Nellie were still waiting for the twins when they came from the school. The children chattered excitedly all the way home.

"This is getting to be more and more mysterious!" Nellie remarked with a little shiver.

When Bert and Nan reached their house they found it in an uproar. "Freddie is lost!" Flossie sobbed when she saw her older brother and sister.

"What has happened, Mother?" Nan asked, stooping down to hug Flossie.

"Oh, Nan, I'm terribly worried," Mrs. Bobbsey began. "Freddie disappeared while he and Flossie were looking at toys. We couldn't find him anywhere!"

Flossie nodded solemnly. "All the people in the store were looking for him."

Mrs. Bobbsey said that she finally decided Freddie had grown tired and had gone home by himself, although he had never done such a thing before.

"But when Flossie and I got here, Freddie hadn't come," Mrs. Bobbsey said in despair. She went on to explain that she had telephoned the store, but by that time it had closed.

"I called your father, and he and the police have been searching all over town. I can't imagine where Freddie could have gone!"

"Where is Dad now?" Bert asked. "Maybe I can help him."

"He was going to walk down to the store and see if he could spot Freddie along the way."

Bert started for the door. "I'll catch up with him," he said.

As Bert reached the door, Mr. Bobbsey walked in. A quick glance at the worried faces told him his little son had not returned. He sank wearily into a chair.

"The police are riding around in the prowl car. They're sure to find Freddie before long," he said, trying hard to appear cheerful.

At this very moment Freddie was waking up in the shipping room of the department store. It was quite dark, and for a moment he could not remember where he was.

"Oh dear," he thought. "I wonder how long I've been asleep. I'd better get upstairs or Mother will be worried about me."

He arose and started forward. *Bump!* He ran into a big box. Then he turned in another direction and stumbled over a barrel.

"It's awf'ly dark and quiet in here. I wonder where everybody is. I guess I'll call someone."

"Help!" he screamed. "Please somebody come and let me out!"

There was no reply, but suddenly Freddie felt something soft rub against his bare leg. For a moment he was so frightened his heart seemed to stop beating. Then he heard a low *purr*.

"It's a kitty!" he cried joyfully, and stooped down. Freddie picked up the cat, which immediately cuddled against his shoulder.

Feeling better now that he had company, Freddie felt along the wall until he came to a door. He turned the knob and stepped out into the basement room where he had been earlier. This was lighted by a dim bulb and, still clutching the cat, he crossed to the other door and soon emerged into the mechanical toy department.

This room, too, was dimly lighted. The counters which earlier had held such interesting toys now were covered with white cloths. This made Freddie shiver and think of ghosts.

"Everyone has gone home and left me alone! I don't want to stay here all night by myself!" he thought desperately.

The little boy wandered over to the model automobiles, but they were all locked and would not move. He bumped into a tall mechanical toy. Its head was mounted on a spring, and it began to move back and forth!

Freddie screamed in fright!

The next moment he heard footsteps overhead, and a man's voice called, "Who's there?" The voice sounded so harsh that Freddie was afraid to answer.

There was silence for a few minutes, then Freddie heard heavy steps descending the stairs.

Not knowing what to do, the little boy crouched behind a counter and peered out.

The man had a flashlight in one hand and a club in the other. Freddie was very still, although his heart was beating loudly. Perhaps this man was a burglar planning to rob the store! Freddie wondered what he should do.

"Must have been the cat," the man muttered as he reached the bottom of the steps.

Now that Freddie could see him better, the little boy decided the man did not look like a burglar. He was bald with just a ruff of white hair around his head, and his face looked very kind.

"Here, kitty, kitty, kitty," the man called.

"Meow!" the cat in Freddie's arms replied.

Quickly the man flashed his light around until its beam fell on Freddie. "Well, bless my soul!" he exclaimed. "What are you doing here?"

Freddie felt braver now and stepped from behind the counter. "I guess I'm lost, and I want my mother," he said with a little catch in his voice.

"You want your mother?" the man repeated. Then he had a thought. "Say, are you the little boy they were looking for all over the store this afternoon?"

"I don't know," Freddie replied. "I was just looking at the toys, then I went in that room over there. I sat down in some soft stuff to rest and fell asleep!"

"Well, bless my soul!" the kindly man exclaimed. "And you've been here ever since? Didn't you know everyone in the store was looking for you?"

Freddie shook his head. "I was asleep," he said, "and Mother says I'm awf'ly hard to wake up!"

"You must be a mighty good sleeper!" the man agreed with a laugh.

"Do you own this store?" Freddie asked curiously.

"No." The man chuckled. "I'm Ryan, the night watchman. You must be Mr. Richard Bobbsey's little boy Freddie."

"Yes, I am, Mr. Ryan, and I'd like to go home now," Freddie replied.

"I'm sure your father will come right down for you," Mr. Ryan said. "Your family will be mighty glad to hear you've been found!"

The night watchman led the way up the stairs to the main floor of the store. Freddie followed, still clutching the black cat in his arms.

"I'll telephone your daddy," the watchman offered, stopping beside a row of telephone booths. "Do you know your number?"

"I can dial it," said Freddie.

At the Bobbsey home Freddie's father had received a report from the police that they had not found Freddie, but were about to broadcast an appeal over the local radio.

Mr. Bobbsey rose wearily from his chair. "Come on, Bert," he said, "let's scout around the neighborhood again."

At that moment the telephone rang. Nan sprang to answer it!

CHAPTER VII

A KITE RIDE

MR. AND MRS. BOBBSEY, Bert, and Flossie listened breathlessly as Nan said hello.

"Freddie!" she cried out. "Where are you? What! We'll be right down!"

Nan turned from the phone, her face radiant. "He's at Taylor's department store."

"Thank goodness!" Mrs. Bobbsey cried.

The whole family piled into the station wagon, and Mr. Bobbsey drove to the store. Freddie and the watchman were standing outside. The black cat was still in Freddie's arms.

"Oh Daddy! Mother! And everybody! I'm so glad to see you," Freddie cried out. "I promise never to get lost again!"

Mr. Bobbsey rumpled his small son's hair. "We're mighty glad to find you, my little fireman," he said. After thanking the watchman for taking care of Freddie, he turned to the little boy.

"All right, put the cat down and hop into the car."

"Oh no, Daddy," Freddie wailed. "The cat is the one who found me! He's my friend!"

Mr. Ryan chuckled. "That's right. They've made friends with each other. I told Freddie he could take the cat home if you have no objection."

"We can't turn down a rescuer!" Mrs. Bobbsey spoke up. "Bring him along, Freddie."

The little boy waved good-by to the kindly watchman and climbed in beside his father. On the way home Freddie told his story of being locked in the big store.

"Weren't you ever scared?" Flossie asked her twin admiringly.

Freddie admitted that it was spooky waking up in a strange place. "But then the kitty came along and I wasn't alone!"

"I've just made up a poem about Freddie," Bert said teasingly. "Listen!" He recited:

"Freddie ran off and down he sat,

A meow woke him up, and there was a cat!"

All the Bobbseys laughed at Bert's rhyme. As they reached home and entered the house by way of the kitchen, Dinah's eyes glowed.

"I'm sure glad you aren't lost any more," she said. "Everybody around here was too worried to eat dinner. I'll bet you're mighty hungry, Freddie. If you all are ready now, I'll put dinner on the table."

"Thank you, Dinah," Mrs. Bobbsey said with a smile.

Later, between bites of crisp fried chicken, Flossie asked, "What's the kitty's name?"

"Mr. Ryan said he didn't have any," Freddie explained. "He just called him kitty."

"Maybe we should call him Taylor after the store," said Nan.

"Oh, that's not cuddly enough," Flossie objected.

"I know," said Freddie. "I'll call him Snoop!"

"Why Snoop?" Bert wanted to know.

"Because he was snooping around the store and he found me!" Freddie said triumphantly.

So the black cat was named Snoop. He was given some raw liver and milk and purred contentedly.

The next morning was sunny and breezy. Mr. Bobbsey came into the yard where the twins were playing ball and asked, "How would you like to fly some kites?"

"Oh, Daddy, that would be super!" Nan cried. "Where can we get the kites?"

"I'll show you how to build them," Mr. Bobbsey offered.

"Great!" Bert exclaimed. "What will we need?"

Mr. Bobbsey thought a moment, then said, "The easiest kind to make is the two-stick type. We'll try them. There is a bundle of laths in the garage. Get those, Bert."

He instructed Freddie and the girls to bring a sharp knife, some glue, paste, and a roll of strong cord. "We'll need paper, too. Have we any crepe paper?"

Dinah had come out onto the back porch and heard him. "Yes, sir, we got red and green crepe paper left over from Christmas. It's on the shelf of Mrs. Bobbsey's closet."

Nan ran to get the paper and the knife while Flossie collected glue, paste, and the cord. Freddie brought out a pencil, a ruler, and a pair of scissors. All of these supplies were placed on the picnic table. The twins' mother joined the group and looked on with interest.

Mr. Bobbsey picked up the laths. "These are just about the right thickness," he said. "Now for each kite, cut one stick twenty-six inches long for the spine or vertical stick; the other, which is the cross, should be twenty-two inches long."

There was much borrowing of pencil, ruler, and knife until the sticks were properly cut. Then Mr. Bobbsey showed the children how to notch a groove in the end of each stick.

"Next, you measure seven inches from one end of the longer stick or spine and mark the spot.

Then glue the sticks together exactly at right angles with the center of the cross stick at the mark on the spine."

Freddie and Flossie had a little difficulty gluing the sticks together, but with the help of Bert and Nan they finally managed it. As soon as the glue was dry, they followed their father's directions and bound the joining solidly with cord.

"Now comes the frame," Mr. Bobbsey said. He showed the children how to tie one end of a length of cord to the top of the spine, then carry it all around the frame through the groove in each stick end.

"Next is the paper," he said. "What colors are you going to use?"

Nan and Flossie decided to make their kites green, while Bert and Freddie took up the red crepe paper. When this was pasted onto the frame, the kites looked very gay.

"They're bee-yoo-ti-ful!" Flossie exclaimed.

"But they're not finished yet," her father reminded her.

He showed them how to make the bridle by fastening two lengths of string to the ends of the sticks and joining them in the middle. Then, exactly where the bridles crossed each other, a piece of string about five feet long was fastened.

"This is the leader," Mr. Bobbsey explained. "You tie the rest of your cord to it whenever you want to fly your kite."

"I'm so 'cited!" Flossie exclaimed. "When can we make them fly?"

"Let's take our kites to Roscoe's field," Bert proposed. Old Mr. Roscoe lived in a small house near the Bobbseys. The field next to his house was no longer cultivated, and Mr. Roscoe allowed the children to play there whenever they wished.

"Come and watch us, Mother and Dad," Nan urged.

So picking up the colorful kites, the Bobbseys made their way to the field. Snoop walked along beside Freddie. Suddenly the little boy stopped.

"Our kites haven't any tails!" he protested. "I want a tail on mine!"

"I know how to make them," Bert spoke up. "We'll need some cord and paper. I'll get 'em and meet you at the field."

In a few minutes he joined his family at the spot. Quickly Bert cut a fifteen-foot piece of cord. Then he made pleated strips of crepe paper and tied them together with the cord.

The others followed suit, and finally four kites with gay tails lay on the ground. "Now you're ready to fly." Mr. Bobbsey smiled.

Freddie tied a long string to his kite leader, then asked, "Shall I run with it until it goes up?"

Mr. Bobbsey, who had in the past shown the older twins how to fly kites, shook his head. "If the kite's right, you don't have to run with it. Just hold it up to the breeze, and the wind will take it."

Freddie did this. The kite went up but darted about in the air until Freddie had a hard time holding onto the cord. A strong gust of wind suddenly snatched it from his hand. Mr. Bobbsey grabbed the string just in time. After a little practice, the kite fliers were enjoying the sport immensely. The twins' parents left a little later and went back to the house.

Presently the wind grew strong once more, and almost took Freddie's kite from his grasp again.

"Wait, I'll help you," Bert called from across the field where he was trying to get his kite up. He tied it to a nearby fence and ran over to Freddie.

"I think you need more weight on the tail," Bert said when he had examined the kite. "I'll tie a stone on it."

As he looked around the ground for one of a suitable size, Flossie cried out, "There goes your kite, Bert. Did you put a stone on it?"

"Why no." Bert looked up at the soaring kite with a puzzled expression. There was something black hanging at the end.

Then Freddie screamed, "It's Snoop! I can see him! Oh, save him, Bert!"

Nan looked toward the fence. There stood Danny Rugg, doubled up with laughter. She ran over to him.

"Did you tie Snoop onto that kite, Danny Rugg?" she demanded, her brown eyes blazing.

"Sure," Danny blustered. "It won't hurt him. He'll have a nice ride!"

"You're the meanest boy I've ever known!" Nan cried as she ran back to join the others.

Bert, Freddie, and Flossie were aghast as they watched the kite soar through the air with Snoop clinging to its tail. Freddie and Flossie began to cry. Just then the kite dipped above an abandoned barn at the edge of the field. Snoop evidently saw his chance to escape. He tore himself loose from the cord and leaped to the roof of the barn!

The four children raced across the field to the old building. Freddie stationed himself under the spot where Snoop was crouched on the roof.

"Come down, Snoop," he called. "Jump! I'll catch you."

But Snoop only moved a little farther up the slanting roof.

"Maybe I can reach him from inside," Bert said. He ran into the old barn. There was a rickety stairway in one corner. Glancing up, Bert could see numerous holes in the roof.

He raced up the stairs to the loft. By standing on his tiptoes he could reach his hand through one of the larger holes. He did this, waggling his fingers and calling, "Here, Snoop!"

But the cat was only frightened by the waving fingers and moved higher. Bert leaned out the window and called to the children below. "Where is Snoop now?"

"He's gone over to the other side," Freddie cried. "Can you get him there?"

"I can't reach him from here," Bert decided.

"I'll have to try some other way." He ran down the rickety steps and outside.

Nan, Flossie, and Freddie were standing by the barn, watching as Snoop stalked about the roof.

"Maybe Mr. Roscoe would lend you a ladder," Nan suggested as Bert surveyed the situation.

"I guess that's the only way I'll get Snoop down," Bert agreed.

Bert ran across the field to Mr. Roscoe's house and knocked on the door. Nobody answered so he knocked again. Finally, after the third time, Mr. Roscoe opened the door.

"Hello, Bert," the old man said. "What can I do for you?"

"Please, Mr. Roscoe, may I borrow your long ladder?"

"Borrow my ladder? What do you want with a ladder out there in the field?"

"Our cat is on your barn roof and can't get down. I'd like to use the ladder to get him."

Mr. Roscoe looked puzzled. "Why can't he get down the same way he got up, eh?"

When Bert explained that Snoop had gone up on the tail of a kite, the old man chuckled. "That's a new one on me. I never knew cats like to fly!"

"May I take the ladder?" Bert asked desperately.

"Why, sure," Mr. Roscoe replied. "It's out

back in the tool shed. Help yourself. But put it back when you're through with it!"

"I will! Thanks!" Bert ran to the tool shed, got the ladder and began to drag it across the field.

The other children saw him coming and ran to help. It took all four of them to get the ladder up to the barn but at last it was in place.

Bert climbed the rungs nimbly. Snoop watched him from the edge of the roof. But when Bert's shoulders reached the top of the ladder and he cautiously put out a hand to Snoop, the cat scrambled farther up the roof!

CHAPTER VIII

TWO BOY DETECTIVES

"OH, SNOOP!" Freddie wailed as he saw the cat evade Bert. "Please come down!"

Bert reached into his pocket and pulled out the ball of cord which he had used on the kite. He set it on the edge of the roof. Snoop could not restrain his curiosity and advanced cautiously.

When he came within reach, the boy's hand shot out and Snoop was captured! Bert carefully backed down the ladder, the cat held securely under one arm.

On the ground again he was greeted by cheers from Freddie and Flossie. Freddie grabbed his pet. "You rescued me, Snoop," he said, "and now Bert has rescued you!"

"Were you scared?" Flossie asked, stroking Snoop's fur and putting her curly head close to look into the kitten's eyes.

Snoop sneezed and shook his head. Flossie giggled. "Snoop is a brave kitty!" she exclaimed.

The four children carried the ladder back to the tool shed and thanked Mr. Roscoe. "So you got the flying cat down!" he said, chuckling at his joke.

After the children had flown their kites awhile, they reeled in the cords, and walked home. As they stepped into the Bobbsey kitchen, the twins were greeted by the delicious odor of baking cookies.

"Would you like to have your cooky sale this afternoon?" Mrs. Bobbsey asked as she passed a plate of ginger cakes. "Dinah and I can make them for you."

"Oh yes," Flossie exclaimed. "Let's have a cooky store, Nan!"

Later at the lunch table the twins told their mother and father about Danny's trick and how Snoop had been rescued from the barn roof. Then the talk turned to the cooky project.

"What can we use for a store?" Nan asked thoughtfully.

"Why not build it out of that big carton the new refrigerator came in?" Mr. Bobbsey suggested. "I think Sam put it in the garage in case there might be some use for it."

"Oh, yes," Flossie agreed. "We can stand inside and make believe it's a real store!"

Bert and Freddie volunteered to help, and after lunch the twins brought the huge carton out onto the front lawn. "See, the back door's already made!" Freddie said, pointing to the opening where the refrigerator had been taken out.

When the big box was set on end, Flossie opened the "doors" and walked in. "We need a window in front," she said, "so we can sell the cookies."

"I'll fix that," Bert offered. He pulled out his pocketknife and cut an opening in the front of the carton down to about three feet from the bottom.

"That's great," Nan said. "We can put the cookies on plates, and maybe Mother will let us bring out the two end tables from the living room to put the plates on."

When Mrs. Bobbsey was consulted she agreed to their using the tables, which Dinah covered with gleaming white shelf paper. In the meantime the cook had fried a mound of golden-brown doughnuts. She rolled them in powdered sugar, then took from the oven several sheets of crisp chocolate and nut cookies.

Nan arranged these on platters and carried them out to the "store." Flossie stood on the sidewalk and surveyed the display.

"We need some dec'rations," she said critically. "It still looks like a box."

Nan joined her little sister on the sidewalk. "I wonder what we could do," she said thoughtfully. Then her face brightened. "I know!" she exclaimed and ran pell-mell into the house.

In a few minutes she was back with a ball of twine, a roll of cellophane tape, and a box of thumb tacks. Flossie watched curiously as Nan cut off a length of cord and began to string doughnuts on it.

"Oh, I see!" she exclaimed. "We can fasten it to the top and let it hang down in a loop!"

Nan nodded. "Then I thought we could tack some cookies on the inside of the back with the tape."

"Oh, that will be bee-yoo-ti-ful!" Flossie cried, clapping her hands.

When Bert came out of the house to see how they were getting along he put up the doughnut string for them. Nan and Flossie busied themselves attaching the cookies to the inside of the carton.

They finished this and stood back to admire the result. "You ought to have a name for your store," Bert observed.

"That's right," Nan agreed. "What shall we call it?"

At this moment Freddie walked up, munching a cake. "Oh, oh, look at the cooky box!" he said teasingly.

"The cooky box!" Nan exclaimed. "That's a good name!"

"Yes!" Flossie jumped up and down in excitement. "Let's call it that!"

Bert went to the garage and got a can of white enamel which Sam had used to touch up some woodwork in the house. Then while the other twins watched, Nan carefully painted THE COOKY BOX across the top of the carton in big white letters.

"I guess you're in business now," Bert remarked as he prepared to return the paint to the garage. "Freddie and I are going over to the old Marden house and look around. We'll see you later."

Nan and Flossie waved good-by to the boys and prepared to start their cooky sale. They decided that since Flossie was smaller, she would stand behind the "counter" and sell the cakes while Nan walked up and down the sidewalk and told passers-by about the project.

"Wouldn't you like to buy some cookies?" Nan asked a pleasant-looking woman who was the first to pass the Bobbsey house. "We're selling them to raise money for our school."

"Why yes," the woman agreed with a smile. "They look delicious." She made her selection, and Flossie carefully wrapped the purchase in waxed paper.

After that several more people appeared and bought cookies. Then for a few minutes no one came by. Nan and Flossie were rearranging the remaining cakes on the plates when they heard a familiar voice.

"What are the dear Bobbsey twins doing today?" it said in sneering tones.

"Danny Rugg!" Nan exclaimed. "Now, don't you cause any trouble!"

"Trouble?" Danny asked in pretended surprise. "Why should I cause any trouble? I just want some doughnuts!"

With that he snatched the string of doughnuts from the front of the stand and ran off!

"Danny Rugg! Come back here!" Flossie cried out.

Snoop had been crouched on a low branch of a tree near by, watching the proceedings. Now as Flossie cried out, he gave a flying leap and landed on Danny's head!

With a yell the bully threw up his hands to defend himself. The string of doughnuts fell to the ground. Snoop jumped down, and in another second Danny was just a spot in the distance!

"That mean boy!" Flossie wailed. "He's spoiled our pretty doughnuts!"

"Oh, well," said Nan with a sigh, "we've sold almost all the cookies." Then she giggled. "At least Danny didn't get any of our doughnuts."

Flossie picked up Snoop, who had settled down at the foot of the tree and was washing his face. "Snoop is a real hero!" she said, giving the cat a squeeze.

Nan counted the money in the little change box. "We've made almost five dollars for the school!" she announced happily.

While she and Flossie were having their cooky sale, Bert and Freddie had reached the old Marden house. Since it was Saturday, the school building was deserted and somehow the quiet made the empty old house seem more mysterious than ever.

"It really looks spooky, doesn't it, Bert?" Freddie remarked.

"Oh, I don't know," Bert said, trying to act very assured. "After all, it's just an abandoned house."

"Are we going in?" Freddie asked.

"Sure," said Bert, taking the key from his pocket. "Maybe we can find a real clue to the things Mrs. Marden lost."

By this time the boys had almost reached the sagging porch. Suddenly Freddie stopped. "Did you hear something, Bert?" he asked.

"Yes, I think I did," Bert admitted.

The boys stood still and listened. Then from above they heard the sound of a shutter being opened.

"Look!" Freddie whispered, pointing to the side of the house. A shutter in a second-floor window slowly swung open, then closed with a bang.

"Stay away from this house!" The warning

was spoken in a harsh voice which seemed to
come from behind the closed blind.

"Come on, let's go!" Freddie urged nervously.
"Someone's in there!"

Bert stood his ground. "Whoever he is, he isn't supposed to be in there. I'm going in and see who it is!"

"Do you think we should?" Freddie asked in a quavering voice.

On second thought Bert decided that perhaps it was not a good idea to take Freddie into the house. After all, they did not know who the intruder might be.

"I'll tell you what let's do," he remarked. "We'll pretend to go away, then sneak back and watch the house to see if anyone comes out."

Freddie looked relieved. "That's a swell idea," he agreed. Then in a loud voice he called, "Come on, Bert! I'm going home!"

"Okay," Bert replied in an equally loud tone.

The two boys walked off. Once out of sight of the house, they hurried around the school building and circled back, approaching the old mansion from the other side. Here they found a crumbling stone wall covered with vines.

Bert pulled Freddie down behind the wall. "We can see both the front and the back of the house from here," he said. "If anyone comes out we're sure to spot him."

The boys made themselves as comfortable as possible. They kept their eyes fixed on the old house. After a little while Freddie grew restless.

"I don't think anybody's coming out," he said. "Let's go home."

At that moment Bert saw the back door of the house open stealthily. Bert poked Freddie. As they watched, a man's figure crept out the door, then made a dash through the hedge at the rear of the property!

Bert stood up. "Come on!" he cried excitedly. "I'm going to tell Mr. Tetlow!"

CHAPTER IX

THE HIDDEN ENTRANCE

"BUT Mr. Tetlow isn't at school today!" Freddie objected.

"I know," Bert replied. "We'll find a telephone and call him up."

The two brothers ran to a candy store across the street from the school. The proprietor, Mr. Marino, was a great favorite of all the children. He was short and plump and had a merry smile.

"Well now," he exclaimed when he saw Bert and Freddie, "what brings you here on Saturday? Do you like school so well you can't stay away?" He chuckled.

Bert was too excited to spend any time in conversation. "May we use your telephone, Mr. Marino?" he asked.

"It's very important!" Freddie put in.

"Go right ahead," the proprietor agreed. "I guess you know where it is."

The boys hurried to the back of the store where the telephone rested on a shelf. Quickly Bert looked up Mr. Tetlow's number and dialed it. When the principal came on the line, Bert explained what they had seen at the old house.

"Stay where you are," Mr. Tetlow said at once. "I'll be right over!"

It seemed to the boys that Bert had just replaced the receiver when Mr. Tetlow drove up outside the store and parked.

"How do you think the man got in?" Bert asked him as they started over toward the Marden house.

"That's what I can't understand," the principal remarked. "There are supposed to be only two keys to the house. I have one and you have the other!"

He took out his key and opened the front door. Everything was quiet as the three stepped into the hall.

"We'll look through all the rooms and check the window locks as we go," Mr. Tetlow decided, turning into the room to the right of the entrance.

Now that a grownup was with them Freddie felt very brave. He ran around the room and peered at each window bolt. They were all securely fastened. The same thing was true in all the other rooms on the first floor.

When the searchers reached the second floor

they found two broken windows. "No one could get in here without a ladder," Mr. Tetlow observed, "and there was no sign of one outside. So I don't think we need worry about these windows."

Returning to the first floor, he bolted the back door on the inside. "No one will be able to get in this door now!" he stated firmly. "Let's take a look at the cellar. Where are the stairs?"

Bert looked startled. "I don't remember seeing any," he replied.

"There's the trap door that Nan saw," Freddie reminded him.

"That's right," Bert agreed. "But we couldn't find any way to open it."

"Show me where it is," Mr. Tetlow suggested. "Maybe I can figure it out."

Bert led the way to the kitchen and pointed out the cracks in the floor where they had seen the trap door. Mr. Tetlow got down on his knees and carefully examined the old boards.

In a few minutes he motioned to the boys. "See these two little holes?" he said. "I think at one time a handle was inserted here. I may be able to pry up the boards."

He took out a pocketknife and opened a screwdriver attachment. He pushed this into the crack nearest the holes and used it as a lever. The board raised a little.

"I think I can get hold of it now!" Bert exclaimed. He placed the tips of his fingers at the edge of the board and pulled. It came up slowly, revealing a flight of rickety-looking steps leading down into darkness.

"I thought we might need a flashlight," Mr. Tetlow said, "so I brought one from the car."

He pulled it out of his pocket and, flashing it ahead of him, descended the steps. "You boys may come down too if you wish," he called back.

Eagerly Bert and Freddie followed. When they reached the bottom of the steps they looked around. As their eyes got used to the gloom, they could make out a little of the cellar from the light coming in one grimy window.

The floor and walls were made of unevenly spaced bricks. The ceiling was so low that Mr. Tetlow was forced to stoop as he walked over to the two windows. The second window had lost its glass and was covered by a wide board which had been wedged into the window frame.

"It's funny that there are windows on only one side," Bert mused, as he walked slowly around the edge of the cellar.

When he reached the side away from the two windows he felt the wall curiously. One section was covered with cobwebby wood. Then he uttered an exclamation! The wall which seemed solid had moved! With a creak it slid to one side!

"A secret entrance!" Bert cried.

Mr. Tetlow and Freddie ran to his side. "By

George!" Mr. Tetlow exclaimed. "You must have touched a hidden spring!"

"But why would Mrs. Marden have a secret entrance to her cellar?" Freddie asked in bewilderment.

Mr. Tetlow laughed. "I don't imagine Mrs. Marden had it put in. She may not even know it's here!"

"Who made it then?" Bert inquired curiously.

"I don't know. But it may have been put in when the house was built. Many of these old houses had secret entrances to take care of runaways who came up from the South."

"What shall we do about it now?" Bert asked.

Mr. Tetlow examined the sliding wall. "I don't think we can do anything without a hammer and some nails. It's not likely that anyone knows about the sliding door, and as long as the house is going to be torn down soon, I think we'll just not worry about it."

Bert closed the secret door, and the three went up into the kitchen again. As Mr. Tetlow led the way to the front door, he said, "You boys did right to call me. I'll notify the police that there has been another intruder in here and ask them to keep a watch on the house."

"Do you s'pose it was the same man you all saw yesterday?" Freddie wondered.

"I don't know," Bert replied, "but at least he won't be able to come in that back door again!"

When Bert and Freddie reached home, they found the rest of the family ready to sit down to supper. They hurried to wash their faces and hands and then slid into their chairs.

"How was the cooky sale?" Bert asked his sisters.

Nan and Flossie launched into an account of their experiences with THE COOKY BOX. When they told how Snoop had foiled Danny's attempt to steal the doughnuts, Freddie laughed so hard he almost fell off his chair.

"Good for Snoop!" Bert cried. "He got even with Danny for tying him to the kite!"

"What did you boys do this afternoon?" Mr. Bobbsey asked when they had stopped laughing about Snoop.

"Bert found a secret intrance to the Marden house!" Freddie announced importantly.

"A secret entrance! Tell us about it," Mrs. Bobbsey urged.

Bert and Freddie described the cellar of the old house and the way in which Bert had discovered the sliding door.

"I'll bet the person who lifted that trap door in the kitchen when we were there yesterday came into the house through that secret entrance!" Nan declared.

"I don't think so," Bert objected. "When I opened it, the wall was covered with cobwebs. It didn't look as if it had been touched for years!"

"I want to see the secret door!" Flossie cried. "Will you show it to me, Freddie?"

Bert answered for his brother. "We'll show you and Nan on Monday, but I think we ought to keep it a secret from everyone else."

"I won't tell anyone," Nan promised.

The rest of the family agreed with Bert that, since the sliding door could still be opened, no one should be told of its existence.

"Mrs. Marden is coming to dinner tomorrow," Mrs. Bobbsey said. "You might ask her about the secret entrance."

"Goody!" Flossie exclaimed. "I like Mrs. Marden!"

"Perhaps by this time she has remembered where she put the cameo and coins," Nan said hopefully.

The next day after church Mr. Bobbsey drove the twins out to the Rolling Acres Nursing Home. It was warm and sunny, and Mrs. Marden was waiting on the front porch. Flossie jumped out and ran up the walk to escort her to the car.

The elderly woman wore a blue coat over a blue-and-white flowered dress. On her white hair was a pretty blue hat.

"You look bee-yoo-ti-ful!" Flossie exclaimed admiringly.

"Thank you, dear," Mrs. Marden replied as Mr. Bobbsey helped her into the front seat.

Flossie climbed in beside her while Mrs. Bobbsey and the other twins sat in the rear seats. When Flossie looked up at Mrs. Marden the little girl's face took on a surprised expression.

"You found it!" she exclaimed.

"Found what, dear?" Mrs. Marden asked, smiling at Flossie.

"Your cameo!" Flossie fingered a small pin at the elderly woman's neck.

For a moment Mrs. Marden looked confused, then she laughed. "Mr. Marden brought this from Italy before we were married, and I've always worn it." She shook her head sadly. "No, I haven't found the antique one. It was set with diamonds and was very valuable."

Mr. Bobbsey saw that the woman was upset and shook his head warningly at Flossie. He changed the subject, and nothing more was said about the lost articles.

Later, however, when Dinah brought in a towering strawberry shortcake for dessert and set it before Mrs. Bobbsey, Bert brought up the subject of the secret door in the cellar of the old house.

"Oh, yes," Mrs. Marden said. "My husband told me that there was supposed to be such a door, but we were never able to find it. Those old houses often had secret doors and cupboards."

The elderly woman looked thoughtful, then continued, "I had a strange dream last night."

"What was it?" Freddie asked eagerly. "I like to dream!"

"I dreamed I was walking up a chimney," Mrs. Marden said. "Wasn't that queer?"

Bert and Nan looked at each other excitedly. Each had the same thought! Could Mrs. Marden have hidden the lost articles in a chimney?

CHAPTER X

CATCHING A GHOST

WHEN Mrs. Marden described her dream about the chimney, Flossie giggled. "Maybe you were Santa Claus!" she said.

Under cover of the laughter which followed, Bert whispered to Nan, "Could this be a clue, do you think?"

"Yes I do."

Later, while Mr. and Mrs. Bobbsey were driving their guest back to the nursing home, the children went into a huddle. Bert and Nan told the younger twins about their suspicion that Mrs. Marden's dream might have something to do with the lost souvenirs.

"You mean they're in the chimney?" Freddie asked excitedly.

"We don't know, of course," Nan replied, "but let's pay special attention to the chimneys tomorrow when we visit the old house." The others agreed and eagerly looked forward to the next afternoon.

At recess time the following day a group of boys stood admiring the newly paved driveway. Its smooth surface sloped gently down to the street.

"That would make a keen place for a roller skate race," Charlie Mason observed to Bert.

"Okay," Bert agreed. "Let's get our skates!"

Several other boys overheard the conversation and said they would like to join the race. Danny Rugg was one of them. They all ran into the locker room and returned with skates.

"You can be the starter!" Charlie called to Nan, who had just walked out of the building with Nellie.

"What shall I do?" Nan asked.

Nellie pulled a handkerchief from her pocket. "Take this," she directed. "Hold it up high, and when you want the race to start, bring your arm down."

Nan practiced a few minutes until she could bring the handkerchief down in a sharp arc. Then she called, "Okay, boys. Are you ready?"

Bert, Charlie, Danny, and three other boys lined up at the top of the driveway. Nan gave the signal and cried, "Go!" The racers started off, arms swinging as their legs flashed ahead left and right.

Ned Brown was in the lead, but Bert soon drew up to him. Then came Charlie, Danny, and the other two boys.

"Come on, Charlie!" Nellie cried while Nan frantically urged Bert to pass Ned.

The driveway was a little narrow for six racing boys. Charlie and Danny drew ahead of Bert and Ned. Then as Charlie put on an extra spurt of speed, one of his skates accidentally touched Danny's left foot.

Danny went down on his back, feet in the air. The cuffs of his slacks fell back, revealing an amazing pair of socks. They were a large checkerboard pattern of orange, blue, and green!

Unable to keep from giggling at the loud socks, Nan and Nellie ran toward the fallen boy. "Are you hurt, Danny?" Nan asked sympathetically.

Danny sat up and took off his skates. He paid no attention to Nan but gazed down to the end of the drive where the other boys were congratulating Charlie on having won the race.

"I should have won!" he exclaimed. "Charlie tripped me on purpose!"

"What a mean thing to say!" Nellie protested hotly. "You know it was an accident!"

By this time the boys were walking back toward the building, and Danny got up. He muttered ungraciously when Charlie said he was sorry that his skate had caused the accident.

"You didn't deserve to win!" Danny said and walked off into the building.

Bert winked at Charlie. "Don't let him worry you, pal. You know he's always a poor loser!"

The twins met by the door immediately after school was out. "Are we going to search the chimneys now?" Freddie asked eagerly as they were joined by Charlie and Nellie.

"We looked at all the fireplaces before," Nellie reminded them. "Do you think we might have missed something?"

Nan told her about Mrs. Marden's dream. "Bert and I think maybe it's a clue," she added.

The six children walked over to the old house, and Bert unlocked the door. Flossie shivered a little as they stepped into the wide hall.

"I hope that man who keeps running away isn't in here now!" she said, her blue eyes as wide as saucers.

"I'm sure no one can get in the house now," Nan told her with a quick hug.

Bert had brought a flashlight and the six children gazed steadfastly up each of the chimneys. Not a brick was loose. "Nothing's hidden in these chimneys," said Bert finally.

"Let's look at the sections that run through the attic," Nan suggested.

"Good idea," Bert said.

The others agreed, and single file they trudged

up the two flights of stairs. When they reached the top of the attic steps they paused and looked around.

"There are four chimneys, two at each end," Bert pointed out. "We can figure out just where they would be and then examine the walls there from the inside."

Nan and Nellie started toward one end of the long room. Suddenly Nellie stopped and pointed. "Look!" she cried. "The trunk!"

"What's the matter?" Charlie asked. "We looked in that trunk when we were up here before."

"I see what you mean, Nellie," Nan spoke up.

"It's open, and I'm sure we put the lid down when we left!"

The trunk which the children had dragged into the middle of the dusty floor still stood there. But the top was up, and the tray had not been replaced.

"I guess our mysterious intruder has been up here," Bert observed.

"Do you think he's looking for Mrs. Marden's things too?" Freddie asked.

Charlie laughed. "If he is, I guess he's not having any better luck than we are."

"We haven't examined the chimneys yet," Nan reminded the others.

"Where are the chimneys?" Flossie asked. "I don't see any."

Nan explained that the chimneys ran up the outside of the house. "But we thought perhaps there might be some sort of secret cupboard or hiding place on the inside."

Bert walked to one of the windows and after a few tugs managed to open it. Then he leaned out and looked along the side of the house.

"The chimneys are about six feet wide on both sides of this window," he announced, pulling his head back into the room.

The children divided into two teams to examine the walls behind the chimneys. But although they felt every inch of the space, they found no sign of any secret hiding place.

When they had done the same thing at the opposite end of the attic without success, they looked at one another in discouragement.

"I guess Mrs. Marden's dream didn't mean anything," Flossie observed dolefully.

Nan could not conceal her disappointment. She had been so sure the dream was a clue. "I don't know where else we can search," she remarked.

"Let's look at those dresses in the trunk before we go down," Nellie suggested. "Mrs. Marden might possibly have put the things in a pocket of one of them."

Whoever had opened the trunk had mussed up its contents considerably. Nan and Nellie took out the dresses one by one and searched the pockets. In one they found a lace glove with no fingers and in another a yellowed dance program.

"Isn't this pretty?" Nellie exclaimed, holding up a dark red satin dress. The material was so stiff that it stood upright when Nellie set it on the floor.

"I'm going to try it on!" Nan cried. Quickly she slipped the costume over her own dress and began to parade around the attic.

Then Flossie and Nellie each put on one of the old gowns. The boys watched for a few minutes, then Charlie said, "Oh, come on, girls, this isn't finding anything. Let's go downstairs."

The girls reluctantly took off the costumes and put them back into the trunk. They closed the lid and started down the stairs.

When the children reached the landing between the first and second floors, they heard a muffled sound. It seemed to come from the cellar.

Flossie stopped short. "What was that?" she whispered in a frightened tone.

Nan put her finger to her lips, and they all tiptoed down to the front door. As they paused there came another *thump*.

This was enough for Flossie. She flung open the door and dashed out of the house. Freddie and the older children followed.

They had not gone far when Bert stopped. "I forgot to lock the door," he said. "I'll have to go back."

Flossie turned to speak to her brother. "Oh, don't—" she began. Then she screamed. "The ghost!" she cried, pointing at the house.

The others looked. One of the shutters on the second floor had been flung open. In the window was a white figure which swayed as they watched!

Flossie started to run, but Nan caught her by the hand. "Don't be frightened, honey," she said. "Nothing is going to hurt you. There is no such thing as a ghost!"

"Are you sure?" Flossie quavered.

"Of course!" Freddie said stoutly. "They're just people dressed up!"

"You're right, Freddie!" Bert declared. "And I'm going to find out who this ghost is!"

"If you're going back into the house, I'm going with you!" Nan announced. "Nellie and Charlie, will you stay with Freddie and Flossie until we get back?"

The friends agreed to wait for Bert and Nan. As the older twins started for the house, the ghostly figure in the window waved its arms and let out an unearthly screech.

Although Flossie called to them to come back, Bert and Nan walked resolutely toward the house. When they reached it, Bert opened the door noiselessly, and they entered the hall. Everything was quiet now.

They stood listening for a moment, then Bert whispered, "Let's go up to that room and see if the ghost is still there."

Nan nodded in agreement. Hardly daring to breathe, they crept silently up the stairs. When they reached the top, Bert pointed to a doorway on their right. Again Nan nodded.

Pausing after each step and hoping that the old floor boards would not creak, they advanced toward the bedroom. The door was open. Quietly they tiptoed into the room. The white figure was still looking out the window. Suddenly, as they watched, it raised its arms in a threatening gesture.

With a stifled giggle, Nan pointed to the ghost's feet. It was wearing sneakers and orange, blue, and green socks!

CHAPTER XI

A RUINED CAMP TRIP

"THIS is going to be good!" Bert whispered. He dashed across the room, and before the ghost could move Bert snatched off the sheet. Danny Rugg stood revealed!

Furious, the bully turned around. "You think you're smart, Bert Bobbsey!" he cried. "But I had you plenty scared!"

"You didn't scare us at all!" Nan replied quickly.

"I'd like to know how you got in here!" Bert said sternly. "Mr. Tetlow gave me a key, but nobody else is supposed to come in!"

"Teacher's pet, aren't you?" Danny sneered. "Well, I don't need any old key. I have my own way of getting in here if I want to!"

Bert looked uncertain. He was afraid that Danny had somehow found out about the sliding door in the cellar. If Danny knew about the secret entrance, perhaps someone else would find it too and take the hidden jewelry and coins.

On the other hand, if Danny did not know about the sliding door, Bert did not want to mention it and so give away the secret.

Nan guessed her twin's dilemma so she spoke up. "You haven't scared us, so you might as well stop playing such silly tricks," she said. Then she walked out of the room.

Bert followed, leaving a crestfallen Danny to pick up his sheet and come along. Once out of the house, Danny ran off toward his home while Bert and Nan joined Charlie, Nellie, and the small twins.

"Did I see Danny come out with you?" Charlie asked in surprise.

Nan nodded, her brown eyes dancing with merriment. When she told the story of the "ghost" in checkered socks, the rest of the children doubled up with laughter.

"The latest style for ghosts!" Charlie gasped.

When the Bobbseys reached home, they ran to tell their mother about the latest "spooky" adventure in the Marden house, and also their failure to find the cameo and the obsidional coins.

"Perhaps you'd better give up the search," Mrs. Bobbsey advised. "Mrs. Marden may not have hidden the things in that house at all!"

"But Mother, we *have* to find them!" Flossie said seriously.

At that moment the telephone rang. Nellie was calling Nan. "Mother and I would like to have you and Flossie come over to supper this evening," she said. "Daddy is bringing home a surprise which he says you will like too!"

Nan ran to ask Mrs. Bobbsey, then came back to the phone. "We'll be over in half an hour," she reported. "Thanks a million."

When she and Flossie reached the Parks home Nellie was waiting on the front porch. "Daddy hasn't come yet," she announced. "I can hardly wait to see what the surprise is!"

At that moment a car drove up to the curb and Mr. Parks got out. A cloth-covered package dangled from his finger. The girls ran down the walk to meet him.

"It looks like a bird cage!" Nan exclaimed.

"You're right." Mr. Parks grinned as he set the cage on a porch table and removed the covering.

Inside the cage was a bird a little larger than a thrush. It had brown plumage, a black-and-white head, and spots of white on its wings and tail.

"Hello there!" a harsh voice said.

"Why, it talks!" Flossie exclaimed in astonishment.

"What kind of bird is it, Daddy?" Nellie asked.

"He's a myna bird," Mr. Parks explained. "A friend of mine brought him from India, and his name is Rajah."

"Hello, Rajah," Nan said, sticking her finger into the cage.

The bird hopped up onto his perch and sat there swinging for a minute. Then he cocked his head and in the same hoarse voice declared, "Rajah eat! Rajah eat!"

"He's hungry!" Nellie exclaimed. "What does he eat?"

Mr. Parks explained that the bird was what is known as soft-billed. "Instead of seeds he eats fruit."

Nellie ran into the house and in a few minutes returned with her mother. Mrs. Parks carried a purple plum and several strawberries on a plate.

She greeted her husband, then poked one of the berries between the wires of the cage. Rajah hopped down from the perch and began to peck at the strawberry.

He stopped for a moment to say, "Hello there! Rajah eat!"

Flossie giggled. "He isn't very polite. He didn't thank you!"

Rajah must have heard her because he stopped

eating and hopped over to the side of the cage. "Much obliged! Much obliged!" he croaked.

Mr. Parks threw back his head and laughed. "At least, Rajah learns quickly," he remarked.

After the myna bird had eaten two berries and half of the plum Mrs. Parks picked up the cage.

"I think we should take Rajah inside," she said. "Myna birds come from warm climates, and we wouldn't want him to catch cold."

While the girls were playing with Rajah, Freddie, lonesome, wandered about the Bobbsey house not knowing what to do with himself. Suddenly he had an idea.

"Bert," he called, running out to the porch, "let's go camping tonight!"

Bert put down the book he was reading and looked out the window. It was warm and sunny. "That's a good thought," he agreed. "We could pitch a tent down by the lake."

When Mr. Bobbsey came home the proposal was put to him. "I don't see why you shouldn't camp out as long as your mother has no objection," he said. "Why not ask Charlie to go with you?"

Charlie accepted immediately, and in a few minutes he appeared with his sleeping bag.

Freddie met him. "Dinah's going to give us our supper to cook!" he said excitedly.

The Bobbseys loved to go camping. Each one

had his own sleeping bag, and they owned several tents. From the third floor storage room Bert brought down a pup tent and sleeping bags for Freddie and himself.

Dinah added to the pile of equipment a package of frankfurters, a can of baked beans, a loaf of bread, a box of cookies, and a large thermos of milk.

When Mr. Bobbsey saw the array he laughed. "If you're going to camp on the lake shore near the lumberyard," he said, "Sam can drive you. He has to make a special delivery of some lumber in Dalton and can drop you on his way."

Sam Johnson was tall and thin, and when he laughed he showed gleaming white teeth. He was very fond of the twins and often helped them with their projects.

Now he rubbed his head and grinned. "Looks like a powerful lot o' gear for one night," he teased. "But let's get goin'!"

The boys carried their equipment out to the big truck. Then they all piled into the cab with Sam. He let them out on the shore of Lake Metoka and drove off.

"The first thing to do is set up the tent," Bert said as the boys carried their supplies to a little clearing among the trees.

"We ought to find level ground," Charlie reminded the others.

They looked around, and then Freddie ran to a spot near the water. "Here's a good place," he called.

The two older boys carried the tent over. They drove the two poles into the sandy ground and stretched the tent over the connecting rope. Freddie helped pound the pegs into the earth. Then they tied the tent ropes to the pegs and stood back to admire their work.

"That looks keen!" Freddie announced.

"The next thing is to build a fire so we can cook our supper," Bert said, starting to pick up pieces of driftwood from the beach.

Freddie and Charlie helped, and in a few minutes they had a small pile of wood. Next they found some stones which they put around the wood. Charlie crumpled up a paper bag which had held the thermos, stuffed it down among the twigs, and put a match to it. In a few seconds a nice fire was burning.

"I'll get the sticks for the hot dogs," Bert volunteered, "and sharpen them."

Charlie busied himself opening the can of beans. He dumped them into a saucepan which Dinah had provided. Then the boys stuck the frankfurters onto the ends of the sticks and held them over the fire.

Soon the aroma of cooking meat filled the air. "Umm! This smells good!" Freddie said, waving his stick around above the fire.

Zzzz! The piece of meat slipped from the stick and fell into the fire.

"It sure does smell good!" Bert teased, laughing at his little brother's dismay. "Here, hold mine, and I'll fix another one on your stick."

When the frankfurters were sizzling and brown, Bert reached for the loaf of bread.

"Wait," Charlie called. "I'll show you how to make toast!"

He picked up three sticks and slit the ends with his pocketknife. Pulling the ends apart he stuck a slice of bread between them. "See! A toasting fork!" he explained.

The boys toasted their bread and put the frankfurters between the slices. Then they sat down around the fire and ate hungrily.

"This is really great!" Charlie announced as he helped himself to more beans.

By the time the boys had cleared up the remains of their meal, it was dark and they were sleepy. They crawled into their sleeping bags and soon all was quiet inside the tent.

Some time later Freddie awakened. There was a rustling noise outside. It sounded as if a person was dragging something along the ground. Cautiously Freddie raised his head and peered out the end of the tent. All he could see were two balls of white fire staring at him!

"Bert!" he whispered. "Wake up!" He pulled at his brother's sleeping bag.

"Wh-what is it?" Bert murmured sleepily. He sat up.

Freddie pointed to the eyes, motionless at the tent entrance. Bert picked up his flashlight which he had placed near by and shone it into the darkness. The light fell directly on a little animal with brownish gray fur. It looked like a tiny bear with a black mask.

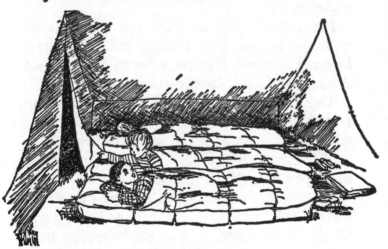

"A raccoon!" Bert exclaimed.

The intruder was motionless for another moment. Then as they watched, it scurried away into the darkness.

"Raccoons are supposed to be very curious," Bert explained. "This one was probably examining our campfire to see if there was anything left to eat."

Freddie snuggled down into his sleeping bag,

and he and Bert were soon fast asleep again. Charlie had slept through all the excitement.

It seemed to Bert that he had been asleep only a minute when he was awakened again. This time the tent was shaking from a strong wind and he could hear the pounding of waves on the lake shore.

"Freddie! Charlie!" he called out. "It sounds as if we're going to have a hurricane!"

The other boys sat up quickly. Above the sound of the waves they could hear the wind howling. Through the tent opening they saw the trees bend with the force of the gale.

"The tent's going!" Freddie screamed.

The boys scrambled from their bags and dashed to the tent pegs. As they struggled to push them deeper into the sandy ground, the storm broke. The rain came down in sheets!

Back at the Bobbsey home, the storm woke Nan from her dream of talking birds. As she got up to close her window she suddenly remembered that her mother had said Bert, Freddie, and Charlie were camping out at the lake.

"Oh dear!" she thought. "The boys will get drenched. The rain will blow right into their tent!"

A streak of lightning and a loud clap of thunder sent her running from the room. "Mother! Daddy!" she called.

Mrs. Bobbsey came to the door of her bedroom. "Did the storm frighten you, Nan?"

"No, Mother, but I'm worried about the boys. Do you think they'll be all right?"

"The wind *is* blowing very hard. I think perhaps your father and I should go get them."

She went back into the bedroom and roused Mr. Bobbsey. In a few minutes the two were dressed and headed for the garage.

"I think I'll take the back road," Mr. Bobbsey remarked as they turned out of the driveway. "It's a little shorter."

"Those poor boys!" Mrs. Bobbsey sighed as she peered through the streaming windshield. "They must be frightfully wet by this time!"

Mr. Bobbsey drove carefully. The driving rain made it difficult for him to see very far ahead, and from time to time branches cracked off the trees and crashed onto the road.

Finally Mr. and Mrs. Bobbsey reached the lumberyard and turned down the narrow road to the lake. "I think they'd probably pitch their tent just to the right here. Can you make it out, Mary?" Mr. Bobbsey asked.

"I can't see a thing, Dick!" she said in a worried tone.

Mr. Bobbsey turned on the distance lights of the car. They shone onto the lake. Suddenly Mrs. Bobbsey caught her breath.

"The tent!" she cried. "It's in the water!"

CHAPTER XII

A MIXED UP GET-TOGETHER

WHEN the rain hit the campers, Freddie, Bert, and Charlie worked frantically to steady the pegs. Fortunately the boys had decided to sleep in their clothes for extra warmth in the cool spring night. But they were soon wet through.

"Get in the tent!" Bert directed. "At least we can stay out of the rain!"

But the wind was too strong for the tent ropes. A particularly violent gust lifted the canvas high into the air. The tent sailed out over the lake!

"Our tent!" Freddie screamed. "It's going in the water!"

The three boys dashed to the edge of the shore. "Maybe we can get it out," Charlie cried.

But the tent was already floating away out of reach. "We can't get it now," Bert said. "Maybe we can rescue it tomorrow."

"Wh-what shall we do now?" Freddie asked

in a shaky voice. He was a forlorn sight as he stood there, water dripping from his hair and face and his clothes plastered to his body by the driving rain.

Bert picked up his sleeping bag. "I guess we walk home," he said wearily.

The other two shouldered their gear and the three boys started off, slipping and sliding on the muddy path. Suddenly they found themselves in the glare of headlights.

The boys stopped, blinded by the strong light. Then a familiar voice boomed out, "Are you all walkin' for your health, or would you like a ride?"

"Sam!" Freddie shouted, sloshing up to the big truck. "Did you come to get us?"

"Not exactly," Sam admitted. He flung open the cab door and helped the shivering boys in. "I'm just on my way back from Dalton. When this rain came up I thought I'd better see how you were makin' out."

"We're sure glad to see you, Sam," Bert said gratefully.

"Your mother and dad are goin' to be mighty glad to see *you!*" Sam said with a chuckle. "I'll drop Charlie off first."

As the truck rolled on through the darkness and rain, the boys peered at the deserted streets.

"There's the school," Bert observed.

Charlie looked past him. "Say," he exclaimed, "isn't that a light in the Marden house?"

"I don't see any," Bert replied, leaning forward to get a better look.

"Sure there is, Bert!" Freddie cried. "I think it's in the kitchen!"

"Who do you suppose it is?" Charlie wondered. "Danny certainly wouldn't be in there in the middle of the night."

"Middle of the night!" Sam repeated. "Why, it's four o'clock in the morning!" He slowed the truck, and they all gazed at the old mansion.

"You're right, Freddie," Charlie agreed. "There is a light in the kitchen. It flickers the way candlelight does."

"Let's go see who's inside," Bert urged.

Sam put his foot on the accelerator. "No, you don't!" he said. "No one's goin' into that old house this time o' morning while *I'm* drivin' them!" He sped on toward Charlie's home.

"I'll call the police as soon as I get in," Charlie promised, "and tell them about the light."

When the truck pulled up at his home the lights were on. Mr. Mason ran down the walk to help Charlie. "I just called the Bobbsey house and Nan said her parents had gone to pick up you boys," he said. "How did you get them, Sam?"

Sam explained about his late delivery trip. "I s'pect Mr. and Mrs. Bobbsey are back home by now," he said.

But when Sam and the boys arrived home they learned from Nan and Dinah that Mr. and Mrs. Bobbsey had not returned.

"They'll be along," Dinah commented. "You boys get upstairs and take hot showers and get into pajamas and robes," she advised. "Nan and I are fixin' you some breakfast."

In the meantime when Mrs. Bobbsey saw the

tent floating on the lake, she was frantic. "Oh, Dick," she cried, "what do you suppose has happened to the boys?"

"Maybe they've taken shelter among the trees," Mr. Bobbsey replied, getting out of the car. The rain was slackening by this time. He took a flashlight from the glove compartment and shone it around.

"I hope they're not hurt!" Mrs. Bobbsey said in a worried tone as she joined her husband.

Together they pushed through the underbrush. Mr. Bobbsey flashed his light over the ground. They examined the area around the camping spot but found nothing.

Finally Mr. Bobbsey paused. "You know, the boys may have started walking home. Let's drive along the regular road."

"All right," Mrs. Bobbsey agreed. "They're certainly not here."

Back at the Bobbsey house Nan was getting worried. "I can't imagine why Mother and Dad aren't back. Do you suppose they've had an accident?"

"I'll go back to the lake and tell them you boys are safe at home," Sam volunteered. He climbed into the truck again and drove off. "I think I'll go by the back road," he told himself.

So while Sam was driving down the short cut, Mr. and Mrs. Bobbsey went along the main road, watching anxiously for any sign of three boyish figures.

They passed no one on the road, and by the time they reached their street Mrs. Bobbsey was more worried than ever. But as they turned into the driveway, she exclaimed hopefully, "Oh, the lights are on in the kitchen! Perhaps the boys are home!"

While all this was going on Flossie had been sleeping peacefully. Now she suddenly awoke. "Nan!" she called, looking across the room at her sister's bed. It was empty!

"Maybe she went to get a drink of water," Flossie decided. She waited a few minutes, but Nan did not return.

Flossie hopped out of bed and put on her robe and slippers. "I'll tell Mother," she thought. Tiptoeing through the hall, she knocked on the door of her mother's and father's bedroom. When there was no answer, she timidly pushed open the door.

No one was in the room. The little girl was bewildered. Where was everyone?

Just then she heard her father laugh. It seemed to come from downstairs. Flossie went to the top of the stairs. There was a light in the dining room.

"Oh, Daddy!" she cried, running down the stairs and into the dining room where her father sat at the table.

"What's the matter, little sweet fairy?" Mr. Bobbsey asked in surprise. "Did you have a bad dream?"

"I can't find Nan anywhere!" Flossie wailed. "I think she's been kidnaped! And I can't find Mommy either."

At that moment Nan, followed by Mrs. Bobbsey, came in from the kitchen. They were carrying platters of bacon and eggs.

"Nan! Mommy!" Flossie exclaimed in relief. "I thought you were both lost! I thought *everybody* was lost—'cept me!"

"Sit down, dear, and we'll tell you all about it," said Mrs. Bobbsey, smiling. She had just finished describing the trip to the lake to look for the boys, when Freddie and Bert came downstairs and seated themselves.

Mr. and Mrs. Bobbsey, Nan, and Flossie listened with breathless excitement as they told of the storm and the sudden end of their camping trip.

"You must have felt like real pioneers," Mrs. Bobbsey remarked to her sons.

Just then Dinah pushed open the kitchen door.

"Sam's back," she announced. "Now you can all stop chasing one another and eat your breakfast!"

Everyone laughed and began to eat hungrily. The clock in the hall struck five. When Freddie had finished counting the strokes, he said with a grin, "I've never eaten breakfast so early before!"

"Nor gone to bed right after it!" his father remarked teasingly. "We can all get a couple of hours sleep before the day really starts."

As they started upstairs again Bert pulled his father back. In a low voice he told of seeing the flickering light in the Marden mansion. "Charlie was going to call the police as soon as he got home."

"That's a good idea," Mr. Bobbsey approved. "Later on we'll find out what happened."

Freddie and Bert fell asleep as soon as their heads touched the pillows. Freddie dreamed that a raccoon was pulling the tent down on top of him. When he opened his eyes he saw that it was Bert trying to wake him up.

"Come on, Freddie," Bert said, "it's time to get dressed for school."

When the twins went downstairs they found that Dinah had a second breakfast ready for them. "It's a long time between five o'clock and lunch," she explained as she set fruit and cereal before the children.

Flossie had just finished the last sip of milk when the front doorbell rang. She ran to answer it. When she opened the door, a police officer stood there.

"Good morning," he said. "Is this the Bobbsey residence?"

"Yes," Flossie replied. "Have you come to tell us something 'citing?"

Before the policeman had a chance to answer her, Mr. Bobbsey came into the hall. "Hello there, Officer Murphy," he called. "What brings you here?"

The policeman explained that Charlie Mason had reported the light in the old Marden house, and had said that the Bobbseys were interested in finding out who the intruder was.

By this time Bert, Nan, and Freddie had joined the group. "Did you find anyone?" Bert asked excitedly.

"No, we didn't," Officer Murphy replied. "We sent two night men over when the call came in. They got a key from Mr. Tetlow and searched the house, but no one was in it."

"I wish we'd stopped and looked ourselves," Freddie spoke up. "Maybe we could've seen if anybody was there."

Seeing the disappointed looks on all the children's faces, the officer added, "Our men did find some muddy footprints on the kitchen floor, however. So someone had sure enough been inside the place."

Bert and Nan looked at each other in bewilderment. Who was the intruder? How had he entered the house? Why was he there?

CHAPTER XIII

A RUNAWAY PET

"WHAT was he doing in the house at that time of night?" Bert questioned. "Do you suppose a tramp might be living there?"

"I don't think so," Officer Murphy replied. "If that were true, we would have found some more evidence of it. As it is, all we saw were footprints in the kitchen."

Mr. Bobbsey walked toward the door with the policeman. "We'll keep an eye on the Marden house and let you know if we catch anyone," the officer promised as he shook hands with Mr. Bobbsey and left.

"Someone else must know about Mrs. Marden's lost treasure," Nan said slowly.

"I think you're right, Nan," Bert agreed. "And he's getting into the house some way to search for the things."

"Oh, I hope he hasn't found the pin and the

coins!" Flossie wailed. "She's 'specting us to rescue them for her!"

"Children!" Mrs. Bobbsey called. "It's time to leave for school! You can talk about Mrs. Marden later."

On the way to school the twins agreed to go through the old house again in their quest for the missing articles.

"If we only had a clue!" Nan sighed.

"Let's telephone Mrs. Marden," Flossie suggested. "Maybe she has thought of something else which would help us."

The others thought this proposal a good idea, so as soon as they came home to lunch Nan put in the call.

"I'm so glad to hear from you," the elderly woman said when she answered the phone. "I've been trying to remember where I could possibly have hidden the heirlooms." She paused, then went on, "Just before I moved from the house I was out in the yard burning some trash, and I'm sure I had the cameo and the box of coins in my pocket then."

"You mean you think you may have burned them!" Nan cried in despair.

Mrs. Marden's voice trembled. "I hope not, Nan," she said. "Perhaps you children could look around the back yard, though. I've searched all my pockets, and the things aren't in them."

Nan promised that the twins would do their best and hung up.

At the lunch table Nan relayed Mrs. Marden's story to her mother and the other twins.

"That's a clue," Flossie remarked hopefully. "Maybe she hid the treasure some place in the yard while she was burning the trash."

"Yes," Freddie agreed excitedly. "Let's dig up the ground!"

Mrs. Bobbsey laughed. "That sounds like a big job. I doubt—"

At this moment Dinah came into the dining room carrying a tray with small dishes of chocolate pudding. She looked worried.

"I been callin' and callin'," she announced, "and Snoop hasn't come for his dinner. He hasn't been around all morning!"

Freddie put down his spoon. "Snoop wouldn't run away," he said in distress. "I'll find him!"

But although Freddie looked under all the shrubbery and up at the low tree branches, he could not find his cat before it was time to go back to school.

Freddie was so busy thinking about Snoop that he could not pay attention to his lessons that afternoon. As soon as classes were dismissed, he told Teddy Blake, the little boy sitting next to him, all about his lovely black cat.

"I saw a black cat going into the woods on the

other side of the road," Teddy said. "Maybe it was Snoop."

Freddie ran up to Flossie as the children were leaving the building and told her what Teddy had said. "Do you want to help me look for Snoop?" he asked.

"Of course," Flossie agreed. "If we go now we can be back by the time Nan and Bert are out of class."

Hand in hand the small twins ran across the road and into the woods. "Here, Snoop! Here, Snoop!" Freddie called as the two children made their way under the big trees.

Freddie and Flossie walked slowly into the woods, stopping to look under low bushes for any sign of Snoop. It was very quiet. Only the twittering of the birds broke the silence.

Suddenly Flossie stopped, her finger to her lips. *"Ssh!"* she said. "Did you hear a cat meowing?"

Freddie listened for a moment, then nodded. "I think it's over this way," he said. He turned to the right and began to run through the woods. Flossie followed.

When they had gone a little distance, Freddie stopped. The meowing was louder now. Flossie grabbed her twin's arm and pointed. There on the lowest branch of a young tree was a tiny black kitten, much smaller than Snoop.

"Here, kitty!" Flossie coaxed. But the black kitten only moved uneasily and meowed louder.

"He's scared," Freddie said. "He's so little he doesn't know how to jump down."

"Let's help him," Flossie proposed. "Can't you get him?"

Freddie stood on his tiptoes but he still could not reach the branch. "I know what to do," he said. "You stand on my back and lift him down."

The little boy got on his hands and knees and his twin stepped carefully onto his back. Then, swaying slightly, she reached up and grasped the black kitten. The next minute she was safely on the ground again, the kitten in her arms.

"It wasn't Snoop that Teddy saw at all!" Freddie exclaimed in disappointment.

"No," Flossie agreed, "but I think this one is lost. Let's take him back to school and see if he belongs to anyone there."

"All right." Freddie turned and walked off.

"That's the wrong way," Flossie called after him. "We came this way." She walked in the opposite direction.

"Oh, Flossie, I don't think so," Freddie said hesitatingly.

The two children stood looking around them uncertainly. Tall trees rose on every side, and all the paths looked the same.

"Which way *did* we come?" Flossie asked, her chin beginning to tremble. "Are we lost?"

"Don't worry, Flossie," her twin said stoutly. "I'll find the way out. Just follow me."

So Flossie, still clutching the kitten, trailed Freddie as he dodged in and out among the trees. In a few minutes she stopped. "We must be lost," she said. "This is the same tree the kitten was in. I'm sure of it!"

Freddie looked discouraged. Then he brightened. "Let's yell," he suggested. "Someone will be sure to hear us."

But, although the twins shouted time after time, there was no reply. They were just about to give up and start walking again when there came a call in the distance. "Freddie! Flossie! Where are you?"

"Here we are!" they called in chorus.

The next minute Nan appeared from among the trees. Flossie ran to her sister. "I'm so glad to see you," she cried. "I thought we would never get out of the woods!"

"Teddy Blake told me you might be here," Nan explained.

"We came to find Snoop," Freddie remarked, "but we found another black kitten instead!"

Nan looked at the kitten in Flossie's arms. "I think that's Susie Larker's Blackie," she said. "Blackie has a white spot under his chin just as this one does."

Susie was a little girl who lived near the school and sometimes played with Flossie and Freddie.

Flossie looked more closely at the black cat. "I'm sorry I didn't rec'nize you, Blackie," she said, snuggling the kitten under her chin. "We'll take you home. Don't you worry."

Nan led the small twins out of the woods. When they reached Susie Larker's house, the little girl ran up to them. "Oh, you've found

Blackie!" she cried. "I was so worried. Mother said he'd surely find his way back home, but he's so little I was afraid he'd forget!"

"I guess cats always remember where they live," Nan agreed. Then she said to Freddie and Flossie, "That gives me an idea about Snoop!"

"What, Nan?" Freddie asked.

"Maybe he went back to that store where you got him!"

Flossie jumped up and down in excitement. "Yes," she cried. "Let's go see if he's there!"

As they passed the school the twins saw Bert playing ball with Charlie Mason and Ned Brown. Nan ran over to tell him where they were going.

"Okay," he said. "I'll wait here for you, and when you get back we can look around the yard of the old house."

"Come on, Bert," called Ned. "It's your turn at bat."

Bert ran off and the other three children started toward the shopping section of Lakeport. They had not gone far when Flossie saw Mrs. Bobbsey driving toward them.

"There's Mother!" she shouted. "Maybe she'll take us to the store."

The car pulled up to the curb. "Where are you children going?" Mrs. Bobbsey asked in surprise. "And where's Bert?"

When Nan explained that they were looking

for Snoop and thought perhaps he had gone back to the store, her mother looked interested. "Hop in," she said. "I'll drive you down and wait while you ask about Snoop."

She parked in front of the store while the three children ran inside.

"I wonder where Mr. Ryan the watchman would be?" Nan remarked.

"He was in the basement when he found me," Freddie reminded her.

"We can go down in the escater," Flossie cried in delight.

Nan saw a tall, dignified man standing by one of the counters talking to the saleswoman. He wore a white carnation in his buttonhole.

"I think he's the manager," she said. "I'll ask him about Mr. Ryan."

When she put her question to him, the man looked at his watch. "Yes, I think Ryan has come on duty. You can probably find him in the shipping room in the basement."

The children rode down on the escalator. When they reached the basement Freddie showed Flossie the mechanical toys and told her how queer they had looked at night when he had found himself locked in.

Finally they reached the shipping room. Freddie spotted his friend the watchman seated in a corner.

"Oh, Mr. Ryan," he called, running over to the man. "Has Snoop come back?"

"Hello there, young man," the friendly watchman replied. "Who might Snoop be?"

"Snoop's the black cat who found me the night I was locked in here," Freddie explained. "You remember—you gave him to me!"

Mr. Ryan got up from his chair and walked over to the children. "Of course! The little black cat! Has he run away?"

Nan explained that Snoop had disappeared during the day and that they had thought he might have returned to his home in the store.

"That's too bad," Mr. Ryan replied sympathetically. "I haven't seen him around here. But if he shows up, I'll let you know right away!"

The children turned away in disappointment and started for the escalator. Then Nan had another thought. Running back to the shipping room, she said to the watchman:

"Excuse me, Mr. Ryan, but can you tell us where Snoop lived before he came to the store?"

"I can't tell you much," the watchman replied slowly. "One day a woman customer was down here, and we got to talkin' about one thing and another. She said she was breakin' up her home and didn't know what to do with her cat. I sort of like company when I'm here at night so I said I'd take him."

"Where did the woman live?" Nan asked breathlessly. "Maybe Snoop went to her house."

Mr. Ryan shook his head. "She brought the cat in and left it. I never knew her name or where she lived."

CHAPTER XIV

HOPEFUL HUNTERS

MR. RYAN did not know who had given him Snoop! The twins were heartsick. They had been so sure they would find the missing cat.

"Where can we look now?" Freddie asked unhappily.

When the children went out to the car, Mrs. Bobbsey had a suggestion. "Perhaps you should advertise in the paper for Snoop. Someone may have found him and not know where he belongs."

Flossie threw her arms around her mother. "Oh, Mommy!" she cried. "That's a wonderful idea!"

So Mrs. Bobbsey drove to the newspaper office. The children ran inside. "We'd like to put a notice in your paper about our lost kitty," Flossie informed a young woman who sat at a desk near the door.

The woman smiled and handed Flossie a pad of paper. "Just print your ad here, and I'll see that it gets in tomorrow morning's paper," she said.

Flossie eyed the paper doubtfully, then passed it to Nan. "You do it, Nan," she urged. "You print better than I do."

So Nan took the pad and after consultation with Freddie and Flossie she printed:

LOST: *Black cat named Snoop. If found please call the Bobbsey twins at Lakeport 2–5135.*

"I hope you find your cat," the young woman said kindly as she took the paper and began to count the words.

The twins thanked her, and when Nan had paid for the ad, ran out to the car again.

"Where to now?" Mrs. Bobbsey asked with a smile as they climbed in.

"We told Bert we'd come back and search around the yard of Mrs. Marden's house," Nan explained.

"All right. I'll take you there," her mother agreed. "But don't stay too long."

When they drove up to the school a little later, the ball game was over and Bert was seated alone on the front steps of the old house.

"Did you find Snoop?" was his first question as the children jumped out of the car and ran over to him.

"No, but he's going to be in the paper tomorrow morning!" Freddie announced importantly.

Nan, Freddie, and Flossie took turns telling Bert what they had done. "It's too bad Mr. Ryan didn't know the name of the woman who owned Snoop," he commented. "The kitten may have gone to the house where she used to live."

"And the people there won't know who Snoop is!" Flossie cried, her blue eyes filling with tears.

"Let's see if we can find Mrs. Marden's lost things now," Nan suggested, trying to get Flossie's mind off the missing pet.

The four children walked to the rear of the old mansion. The back yard was about the same size as the one at the Bobbseys' home. It was bordered at the back and on one side by a tall hedge. On the other side near the rear was a small tool house and beyond it stretched an open field.

"Maybe she buried the jewelry and coins somewhere near the porch," Bert suggested.

They carefully examined the rickety steps and the ground around the sagging porch, but found nothing. Then Freddie picked up a stout stick and began to dig around the roots of the hedge. After a few minutes Flossie found another stick and went to help him.

"I've found something," she called after digging for a short while.

The other three ran over to see. But when

Flossie succeeded in uncovering the object it turned out to be only a red brick.

Nan began to wander around the yard. Finally she stopped at a spot near the tool house. "This must be where Mrs. Marden burned her trash," she called to the others.

When they joined her, Nan pointed to a bare area in the lawn. There were little bits of glass and wisps of half-burned cloth on the ground. Bert bent down and carefully poked around in the debris.

"Do you s'pose the things fell out of Mrs. Marden's pocket and burned up?" Flossie asked fearfully.

"I don't think the cameo would burn," Bert observed, "and certainly not the coins. Part of the metal might melt but there would be something left."

"Do you see any signs of it?" Nan asked, crouching beside her twin.

He shook his head. Although the four children sifted the ashes through their fingers, they found nothing that resembled the cameo or any kind of metal.

Next they looked in all the forks of the trees which they could reach and searched the ground for any signs of fresh digging. But they found nothing.

"Well, I guess the tool shed is the only place left to look," Bert said in discouragement.

The little house was so small that all four children could not get in at once. It was decided that the younger twins would search the shed first.

This proved to be a real task. The space around the edge of the floor was filled with cans and buckets of dried-up paint. On the wall hung rusty garden implements covered with cobwebs.

Across the back wall was a low shelf. Freddie picked his way through the junk and began to examine the things on the ledge. "Here's something way back in the corner!" he exclaimed. He stretched his arms as far as he could and managed to take hold of a box. He carried it out into the sunlight.

"It rattles!" Freddie exclaimed triumphantly.

"Oh Freddie! I think you've found the treasure!" Flossie jumped up and down in excitement.

Bert and Nan watched breathlessly as Freddie pried up the lid of the old cigar box. Then they leaned forward to see what was inside.

"It's only some bolts and screws!" Bert said in disgust.

This second disappointment was too much for Flossie. "I'm tired," she said forlornly. "Let's go home."

"We might as well," Bert agreed. "I don't think we're going to find anything here today."

The twins were so quiet during supper that Mrs. Bobbsey was worried. "You children

mustn't take this search for Mrs. Marden's heirlooms so seriously," she cautioned. "I'm sure
they'll turn up sometime."

"That's right," their father agreed. "And
Snoop will be back when he gets hungry!"

Freddie cheered up a little at this remark.
Then Nan said, "I know what let's do tonight.
Let's have a movie show!"

"How can we do that?" Flossie asked, her face
brightening.

"We'll have to wait until it gets dark. Then
I'll show you," Nan replied.

Mr. and Mrs. Bobbsey were going out for the evening so they said good-by shortly. "Don't stay up too late, children," Mrs. Bobbsey said. "Remember tomorrow is another school day."

The twins played in the back yard until it grew dark, then they all went into the living room. Nan brought in Sam's large flashlight which he used when working on the car. She hooked it over the back of a chair and directed Bert to turn out the other lights.

When the room was dark Nan snapped on the flash and focused it on one wall. It made a round glowing spot.

"Now watch," she said. She put a handkerchief over one hand, then with the fingers down like little legs she held her hand in front of the light. It threw a shadow on the wall.

"This is Little Red Riding Hood," she explained, wiggling her fingers until it did indeed look like a little girl hurrying along. "And this is the wolf!" She moved her other hand so that the shadow was a wolf sneaking after Red Riding Hood.

"Oh, Nan, that's bee-yoo-ti-ful!" Flossie cried. "Let me do one!"

So all the twins took turns making moving pictures with their hands. Flossie made two little rabbits. "See them hippity-hop along," she said. Freddie's movie was of the tortoise and the hare.

One hand hopped as the hare while the "turtle" crept slowly.

Bert made a dog with long floppy ears.

"Meow, meow!" cried Flossie. "I'm a cat. Chase me!"

Bert jumped up to put his hand next to hers. As he did he knocked the flashlight off the chair back. It landed with a crash and the room was plunged into darkness!

Bert ran to turn on the room light and survey the damage. "I hope Sam's flash isn't broken," he said in a worried tone.

Nan picked it up. "It's all right," she observed. "The bulb was just knocked loose. See!" She tightened the bulb and the light came on. "And now we'd all better go to bed."

"Making shadow movies is fun," declared Flossie to her twin as they went upstairs.

Freddie nodded. Then he said, "I hope lots and lots of people read the paper tomorrow, and see our ad about Snoop."

"I do too," said Flossie. "I think we'll hear something," she added confidently.

Flossie was right. The twins had been home from school only a short time the next afternoon when the telephone rang. Nan hurried to answer it.

The others heard her say, "Oh, thank you so much. We'll come right over. The address is twenty-one Maple Street? Yes, we can find it. Good-by."

When Nan came back into the living room her face was beaming. "It sounded like a very old lady," she announced, "but she says she has Snoop, and we may come and get him! Isn't that wonderful news?"

"Goody! Goody!" Flossie cried, clapping her hands. "Snoop is found!"

Freddie was so jubilant he did three somersaults in a row on the living room floor.

Bert started for the door. "I know where Maple Street is," he said eagerly. "Come on everybody! Let's go!"

Nan hesitated. "I'm sorry Mother isn't home to take us, but I'm sure she won't mind if we go. I'll tell Dinah."

Maple Street proved to be rather a long way from the Bobbsey home, but the children were excited at the prospect of finding Snoop and so hurried across town. As they turned into Maple Street they began to look for number twenty-one.

Finally Nan stopped, a puzzled look on her face. "This can't be the right place. It's a fur store."

"It's twenty-one," Bert remarked. "Let's go in anyway."

As Flossie followed the others into the shop she suddenly stood still. Her face turned white.

"Oh no!" she cried. "They didn't make that out of our lovely Snoop!" She pointed to a black fur piece draped over a chair.

Before Nan could reassure her little sister, an old man came from a back room. "Don't you make fun of my furs!" he shouted, scowling and pointing his finger at Flossie.

"My sister didn't mean that," Nan said quickly. "Someone telephoned that our black cat Snoop had been found and was at this address."

"Yes," Freddie spoke up. "We want Snoop! Will you please give him to us?"

To the twins' utter astonishment, the man's face turned red with rage. "I don't know anything about any telephone call or any cat named Snoop!" he yelled. "Get out of my shop, you meddlesome kids! Get out!"

CHAPTER XV

A NEW CLUE

"COME on!" Nan said to her brothers and sister when the irate man ordered the twins to leave his shop. "I'm sure Snoop isn't here!"

Outside on the street again, the children looked at one another in astonishment. "Well!" Bert exclaimed with a gasp. "That phone call must have been a fake!"

"Ooh! Wasn't that man in the store awful?" Flossie shuddered. "I'm glad he didn't find Snoop!"

"I agree with you, Bert," Nan stated. "The call was a fake. And I've a good idea who made it!"

"Who?" Flossie's eyes widened.

"I know!" Freddie exclaimed. "Danny Rugg!"

The twins concluded that Danny had made the call to play a trick on them. Bert guessed that the bully had probably seen the advertisement in the morning paper and had hurried home from school to telephone the Bobbseys.

"I wish we could fool Danny some way," Freddie said as they began their long walk home.

"Yes," Flossie added. "He's always playing mean tricks on us!"

"Let's try to think of something," Bert suggested.

For a short while everyone was silent, trying to think of a way to outwit Danny Rugg. Then Flossie began to giggle.

"What are you laughing at?" Freddie asked. "Have you thought of something?"

Flossie outlined her plan. When she had finished Bert chuckled. "That's great, Flossie!" he exclaimed. "Let's do it!"

"But Flossie and I won't be able to see what happens!" Freddie objected.

"If it works out right, we'll tell you all about it," Nan promised.

"Okay," Freddie agreed reluctantly.

When the twins reached home Flossie ran upstairs but came down again in a minute with a small fur muff in her hands. "This is the one I meant," she explained to the others. "It belonged to my big dolly that got broken. We can use it."

"That'll be keen!" Bert observed with a grin.

"Just perfect!" Nan put in.

"And here is the hot water bottle!" Flossie pulled a little one out of the muff. "It came from my dolly's medicine kit."

While all the twins were laughing about the trick they planned to play on Danny at school the next day, Mrs. Bobbsey came into the room. She had several books under her arm.

"I'm going to take these over to Mrs. Marden," she said. "Would any of you like to go with me?"

"I'll go!" Flossie cried.

"So will I," Nan said.

The boys decided to stay at home. Bert said he had promised to help Freddie repaint his toy fire engine. "This would be a good time to do it," he added.

"That's a swell idea," Freddie agreed. "Then it will be dry by tomorrow in case I need it!"

After Mrs. Bobbsey and the girls had left, Freddie carried his fire engine out to the garage. Bert was examining a can of red paint.

"I think there's just about enough here," he decided.

They set to work, and the paint job was soon finished. Freddie put the gleaming engine on a shelf to dry, then turned to Bert.

"Why don't we go down to the lake and see if we can find our tent?" he suggested.

"Okay," the older boy agreed, and the brothers started out.

When they reached their camping site, Bert and Freddie scanned the near-by shore for any sign of the tent but without success.

"It may have drifted to shore some other place," Bert said. "I'll ask Dad if we may take out a boat and look for it."

The boys walked up to the lumberyard office. Mr. Bobbsey was busy talking on the telephone when they went in. He motioned for them to sit down and went on with his conversation.

In a few minutes he put down the receiver and turned to his sons. "Well, boys," he said, "what brings you here?" He chuckled. "Another mystery up your sleeve?"

Bert explained that they hoped to find their tent and asked his father if they might use one of the lumberyard boats for their search.

"Find Sam," Mr. Bobbsey suggested, "and ask him to take you in the motorboat. I don't think he's too busy just now."

"Thanks, Dad," Bert said.

The two boys went out into the big lumberyard and looked around for Sam. In a minute they spotted him. They ran over, and Freddie explained what their father had said. Sam grinned broadly, showing his white teeth.

"They sounds good to me!" he exclaimed.

"It's a right nice sunny day for a ride on the lake."

He led the way to the boathouse, and in a few minutes the three were in the motorboat cutting through the clear, sparkling water of Lake Metoka. Sam steered the boat back and forth near the spot where the boys had camped.

"I don't see anything," Freddie said presently. "Do you think the tent sank to the bottom of the lake?" he asked despairingly.

"Maybe," Sam admitted. "But it might have caught on something underwater and not be far down."

"How can we get the tent if that happened?" Bert asked.

Sam turned the motorboat back toward the shore. "There's a hook in the boathouse. I'll get it."

When they reached the dock he threw a rope over a post and hopped out. "I'll be right back," he called as he ran toward the boathouse. The boys waited.

Sam returned in a few minutes carrying a long pole with an iron hook on the end. "You can drag this in the water as we move along," he explained. "It may catch onto the tent."

"I get it," said Bert. "We'll dredge for the tent."

Once more the boat put-puted out onto the

quiet lake. Only an occasional fish coming to the surface for a nibble disturbed the glassy calm. "The lake doesn't look the way it did the other night, does it, Sam?" Bert remarked with a smile.

"Boy, it sure was rough then!" Sam exclaimed. Then he laughed. "And I never saw three boys any wetter!"

"May I dredge now, Sam?" Freddie asked eagerly.

Sam nodded and handed the long pole to the little boy. Then he showed him how to hold the pole down over the side of the boat so it would catch anything under the water.

Slowly Sam steered the boat parallel to the shore about twenty feet out. They went up a half mile in one direction, then turned.

"There's no tellin' where the wind took that tent," Sam observed, "but it shouldn't be too far away from where it went out."

At that moment the hook caught onto something. Freddie was holding the pole very tightly and when it stuck, he was pulled off balance. Bert made a lunge and caught Freddie's legs just as he was about to go over the side!

"Wow! Thanks, Bert!" Freddie cried after his brother had dragged him back into the boat.

"You think you were goin' for a swim?" Sam teased.

Freddie grinned. He still clutched the pole.

Freddie was about to go over the side

Now he remembered what had caused his upset. "I snagged something!" he cried. "Turn around and go back, Sam!" he pleaded.

Obligingly Sam made a turn and in a few minutes came over the spot again. Bert and Freddie both held the pole while the boat moved slowly along.

"Stop!" Bert called. "I think we have it!"

While Sam idled the motor the boys carefully pulled up the pole. There, caught on the hook, was the sodden pup tent!

The wet canvas was so heavy that Sam pulled it in while Bert held the boat wheel. Finally the dripping mass was deposited on the deck of the motorboat.

"I don't think it's hurt a bit!" Freddie cried. "But it's sure wet!"

"We'll hang it up at the lumberyard until it dries," Sam told the boys.

In the meantime, Mrs. Bobbsey and the girls had reached the Rolling Acres Nursing Home. Mrs. Marden was very glad to see them.

"Thank you so much for the books, Mary," she said. "Won't you all come up and see my room?"

Nan and Flossie followed their mother and Mrs. Marden up the wide stairs and into a large, sunny room. They looked at a photograph album which Mrs. Marden gave them while the two women chatted.

Finally Mrs. Bobbsey rose. "We must be going home now," she told their hostess.

"But it's not late," Mrs. Marden protested, raising her arm to look at her wristwatch. A startled expression came over her face.

"Is something wrong?" Nan asked.

"My watch!" Mrs. Marden exclaimed. "It's gone!"

"Are you sure you had it on this afternoon?" Mrs. Bobbsey asked.

"Oh, I think I did," the elderly woman said anxiously, "but perhaps I put it some place else."

While Mrs. Marden looked in the drawers of her bureau, Mrs. Bobbsey and the girls searched the tables and shelves. Suddenly Flossie pointed to the door handle.

There, dangling from it was a gold watch bracelet!

Mrs. Marden looked embarrassed. "Now how do you suppose it got there?" she mused. "You girls are very good at solving mysteries. Thank you."

"We have a new mystery to work on!" Flossie exclaimed. "But we're not having any luck solving it."

"What is that, dear?" Mrs. Marden asked, smiling.

"Our kitten has disappeared!" Flossie replied sadly.

"That's too bad," their hostess said sympathetically. "I had a kitten once. I was very fond of him, but when I moved I had to give him away." She sighed.

"Did you give him to some friends of yours?" Flossie wanted to know.

"I can't remember." Mrs. Marden shook her head sadly. "I'm sure I must have. I do hope he has a good home. He was a beautiful black kitten and so loyal to me!"

Flossie and Nan looked at each other in excitement. This description certainly fitted their own pet. Could Snoop have been Mrs. Marden's cat?

CHAPTER XVI

THE TWINS' TRICK

NAN and Flossie were excited to learn of the black kitten Mrs. Marden had once owned. They could hardly wait to get home and tell Bert and Freddie about their idea that the pet might be Snoop!

"That's a swell clue," Bert commented when the girls told their story at the supper table. "A cat likes to go back to his first home, and if Snoop is Mrs. Marden's cat, then maybe Snoop is at the old Marden house!" he ended triumphantly.

Mr. and Mrs. Bobbsey laughed at Bert's long sentence. "Very good reasoning, son," Mr. Bobbsey remarked. "Spoken like a true detective."

"Let's go to school early tomorrow morning," Nan suggested excitedly, "and look around the old house for Snoop!"

"But we've already searched the house!" Freddie objected.

"We haven't been inside since Snoop went away," Flossie reminded her twin.

"And he could be hiding outside somewhere," Bert added.

So the next morning the twins started off to school at an earlier hour than usual.

"Do you have the things for Danny?" Nan asked Bert as they walked down the street behind Freddie and Flossie.

For answer her twin held up a brown paper bag. "All here," he replied, grinning.

When the children reached the old house, everything seemed quiet. A few boys and girls who had also come early were playing in the school yard. But the Marden mansion and the grounds around it were as deserted as ever.

The Bobbseys ran around the yard, peering under bushes and calling, "Here, kitty, kitty!" Every once in a while they paused and listened hopefully for an answering *meow*. But there was no sign of Snoop.

Finally Nan said, "I guess he isn't here after all. And maybe Snoop wasn't the kitten Mrs. Marden gave away."

"We haven't looked in the house," Freddie suggested.

"How would a cat get in?" asked Flossie.

"We might as well look," Bert remarked. "Cats can get in places no one would ever expect them to." He opened the front door with his key, and the four children walked into the hall.

Once more they went through the house, this time paying special attention to the closets and any small spaces into which a kitten might crawl. But they had no success.

"There's still the third floor," Bert said. He and Nan trudged up the narrow stairs to the attic, but Freddie and Flossie did not want to go. "See you later," the little boy called.

The small twins ran down to the first floor. They were chasing each other through the musty, vacant rooms when suddenly there came a loud *meow!* The small twins stopped and listened. The sound came again!

Flossie put her finger to her lips. "I think the —the cat's in the living room," she whispered.

The two children tiptoed across the hall and into the empty room. There was no cat in sight. Then they heard another loud *meow* followed by a snicker. The sound seemed to come from just outside one of the shuttered windows.

"That wasn't any cat!" Flossie declared.

She crept to the window and peered through the blind. She beckoned Freddie to join her. What they saw made the two children giggle. Then together they let out a "meow!" at the top of their lungs.

There was a scrambling noise under the window. Through the shutter Freddie and Flossie saw Danny Rugg running pell-mell toward the school!

"He was trying to make us think he was Snoop, but we scared him! We scared him!" the twins howled with glee.

"Serves him right!" Freddie added.

At that moment Nan called from the kitchen, "Bert! Flossie! Freddie! Come here!"

The younger twins hurried toward the sound of her voice, and Bert came running down the stairs. The four met in the old kitchen. Nan stood in the middle of the room, a paper in her hand.

"Look what I found!" she exclaimed, holding out a small folder.

"Why, it's the last School Assembly program!" Bert exclaimed. "How did that get here?"

"I can't imagine!" Nan replied. "It certainly wasn't here the other time we searched the kitchen!"

Bert passed the paper to Freddie, who looked at it closely. "Look!" he said. "There's a drawing on it."

"Where?" Nan asked. Then as she bent to examine the program, she exclaimed, "I think it's a plan of this house, isn't it, Bert?"

"It sure is!" her twin agreed. "But what's it all about?"

"Someone connected with the school must have been in here!" Nan said. "Do you think it could have been Mr. Tetlow? After all, he has the only other key."

Bert looked thoughtful. "I think we ought to tell him about what you found anyway. Why don't you take the program to him while I fix Danny's surprise?"

"We didn't find Snoop." Flossie sighed. "But maybe Nan found a clue."

There was only a short time before the first bell would ring, so the four Bobbseys walked over to the school. At the door they met Charlie and Nellie.

In low tones Bert and Nan explained about the trick they were going to play on Danny. Charlie guffawed. "That's terrific!" he exclaimed. "I'll help you get it ready, Bert."

The two older boys went off to the locker section while Freddie and Flossie said good-by and turned toward their first grade room.

"I'll see you in a few minutes," Nan said to Nellie as she left her friend and walked down the hall to the principal's office.

"Don't be late for the fun!" Nellie called after her.

"Oh, I won't!"

Mr. Tetlow was at his desk and motioned to Nan to come in when she entered the outer office. He took the program from her and listened intently as she explained that she had found it in the kitchen of the old house.

"This is most disturbing," he observed. "I'm the only person besides Bert who is supposed to have a key, and I haven't been in the Marden house for a week or so!"

"Who do you suppose dropped the program, and why is there a map of the house on it?" Nan wondered.

"I don't know, but I'll turn this over to the

police," Mr. Tetlow promised. Then he looked at his watch. "You'd better get to your classroom. The bell will be ringing in a few minutes."

Nan thanked him and ran down the hall where Nellie was waiting. The two girls walked into class together.

While Nan was in the principal's office Bert and Charlie had gone to the boys' locker room. There they had met Ned Brown and told him what they were planning.

He chuckled and asked, "Can I do something to help out?"

"You can keep Danny out of the way until we have everything ready," Bert suggested.

At that minute Danny Rugg walked into the room. When he saw Bert he sneered, "Aren't you the early one today! I thought you Bobbseys were still playing house or some of your other silly games."

Bert pretended to be busy at his locker and did not reply.

"Say, Danny," Ned called, "I saw your baseball bat over in the corner of the gym a little while ago. You'd better get it before Mr. Tetlow finds it."

"That's right," Charlie chimed in. "You know we're supposed to keep our equipment in here."

"I don't know how it got there," Danny said, "but I suppose I'll have to get it or old Tetlow will be on my neck!" He grumbled and strolled out of the room.

"Good for you fellows," Bert said. "That was a neat way to get Danny out of here." He had been running the hot water in the hand basin. Now he tested it. "That should be about right!" he remarked.

Bert carefully filled the doll's hot water bottle and slipped it into the fur muff. The three boys then walked across the hall and into their homeroom.

The teacher, Miss Vandermeer, was writing on the blackboard and did not turn around when Bert, Charlie, and Ned entered.

Casually Bert walked over to Danny's desk and slipped in the muff. Then he took his seat.

In a minute Nan and Nellie came in. Nan stopped by Bert's desk. "Is everything fixed?" she whispered.

Bert winked and made a circle with his thumb and first finger. Nan giggled and went on.

By this time most of the children were in their places. Just as the final bell rang Danny slipped into the room and hurried to his desk.

After Miss Vandermeer had said good morning to the class, she directed the boys and girls to take out their notebooks and pencils. "I want to give you your assignments now," she remarked.

The eyes of the Bobbseys and their friends were on Danny as he put his hand into his desk!

CHAPTER XVII

A CONFESSION

"OW!" Danny yelled and slammed down the desk lid.

"What is the meaning of this?" Miss Vandermeer asked sternly as a wave of titters spread through the room.

"I—uh—I stuck my finger," Danny answered, his face red.

"I'm sorry if you hurt yourself," the teacher remarked, "but please don't make so much noise. Now take out your notebook and pencil."

But Danny did not move. He sat staring straight ahead.

"Danny!" Miss Vandermeer prompted him, frowning. "What is the matter? I expect an answer when I ask you a question."

Danny gulped miserably. "I—I think there's a cat in my desk!" he finally stuttered.

"A cat!" the teacher gasped in astonishment. "The very idea! Take it out at once!" she commanded.

Gingerly and reluctantly Danny put in his hand and slowly pulled out the muff! He turned a vivid scarlet as the class burst into roars of mirth. Even Miss Vandermeer could not keep from laughing.

"I didn't put it there!" Danny cried. He pointed at Bert. "I'll bet he did it. He's mad at me because I found out he squealed to Mr. Tetlow when I broke that window!"

"He did no such thing," came a voice from the doorway. It was Mr. Tetlow! "Bert would not say who threw the ball," he went on, "but I saw you running away so it was not hard to guess who the culprit was!"

Danny shuffled his feet and looked at the floor. Mr. Tetlow spoke to Miss Vandermeer for a few minutes, then left the room.

"*Did* you put the muff in Danny's desk, Bert?" Miss Vandermeer asked.

Bert looked sheepish. "Yes, Miss Vandermeer," he admitted. "Danny's always playing tricks on me and my brother and sisters, so I thought I'd play one on him!"

"The classroom is no place for tricks," the teacher replied. But a little smile played about her lips. "I will keep the muff in my desk until noontime. You may pick it up then. Now I suggest we get on with our assignments."

With a few suppressed giggles the boys and girls bent over their notebooks and settled down to work.

Shortly before noon a message came for Bert and Nan to report to the principal's office. "I suppose he's going to punish me," Bert said to his twin as they walked down the hall, "but it was worth it to see Danny's face when he felt that muff!"

Nan laughed. "Wasn't he priceless?" Then she added, "I don't think Mr. Tetlow wants to see you about that or why would he want me to come too?"

As Nan suspected, the principal did not mention the muff incident. Instead he indicated a roughly dressed man who was standing near by with Officer Murphy.

"I thought perhaps you children would like to see the man who has caused all the strange happenings at the old Marden house," the principal remarked.

Seeing the twins' puzzled expressions, he went on, "This is Jack Ringley, who used to be a janitor here at the school. We let him go when he began taking supplies."

"But why would he be in the house?" Nan asked in bewilderment.

"Ringley overheard you telling your friends about the missing articles you were trying to find for Mrs. Marden. He decided to look for them himself."

"How did he get in?" Bert wanted to know.

"That's what I wondered," Mr. Tetlow said. "Ringley has confessed that he took the key from my desk drawer one day when the office was empty. He had a duplicate made so he could go into the house any time he wanted to. He returned the key before I had a chance to miss it."

At this point Officer Murphy spoke up. "I've been watching that house. This morning I saw you children leave. Then a little while later this fellow walks up and lets himself in with a key!"

"Then you didn't know about the secret entrance in the cellar!" Nan exclaimed in satisfaction, turning toward the prisoner.

"What secret entrance?" Jack Ringley asked sullenly.

Nan did not reply but Bert burst out, "Was it you who went down through the trap door in the kitchen one day when we were in the house?"

"Yes. You almost caught me that time. I had to duck down there when I heard her"—he nodded at Nan—"coming toward the kitchen."

"I'll bet you took up that lower step too!" Bert said accusingly.

"Sure I did," Jack Ringley replied boastfully. "I wanted to scare you kids so you wouldn't hang around the house while I was looking for those things." Then he added resentfully, "I yelled at you from the upstairs window too, but it didn't do any good!"

"You must have looked in the trunk in the attic. Did you find anything?" Nan asked curiously.

The man shook his head in disgust. "No, I thought I had really found the hiding place when I saw that trunk but there was nothing in it but a lot of musty old clothes!"

The former janitor confessed that he had even

gone into the house very late one night to search for the valuable heirlooms but had not been able to find them.

"That must have been the night Sam drove us home from the lake!" Bert cried. "We saw the light."

Mr. Tetlow took the school program from his desk. "I guess you dropped this on one of your trips," he said.

Then he nodded to Officer Murphy. "That's all. Take him down to police headquarters now. We've found out what we wanted to know. The mystery of the haunted house is cleared up!"

After the officer had left with Jack Ringley, Mr. Tetlow stood up. "Well, it looks as if Mrs. Marden's heirlooms are not going to be found. The wreckers are starting to tear down the old mansion this afternoon."

"I guess the things are not there if none of us could find them," Nan agreed sadly. She and Bert left the office.

Freddie and Flossie had gone home to lunch and were waiting impatiently for the older twins when they finally came to the table.

"We thought you'd never come!" Freddie cried. "How did the trick work?"

"Was Danny scared?" Flossie asked.

Bert and Nan had been so excited about the capture of the mysterious visitor to the Marden mansion that they had almost forgotten about the trick they had played on Danny.

But now they gave a step by step account of what had happened in the classroom. When they came to the part where Danny had pulled the warm muff from his desk, Freddie and Flossie collapsed in giggles.

Dinah had stayed in the dining room to hear the story. She threw up her hands and rolled her eyes to the ceiling. "Hee, hee! That boy sure got what he deserved!" she cried, her ample bulk shaking with laughter.

"I hope that will discourage Danny for a while," Mrs. Bobbsey said, wiping the tears of mirth from her own eyes. "But why are you children late to lunch?" she asked.

"The ghost in the haunted house has been caught!" Bert announced with a grin.

"Who was it?" Freddie asked, so excited he stopped eating his dessert.

Bert and Nan took turns telling of the happenings in Mr. Tetlow's office. Freddie's and Flossie's eyes grew big as they heard of Jack Ringley's confession.

"Then Danny didn't play all those tricks!" Flossie exclaimed, amazed.

"Not all of them," Bert admitted, "but we did catch him playing ghost!"

When the younger twins heard that the old

Marden house was going to be torn down that afternoon they were sad.

"And we haven't found Mrs. Marden's nice things!" Flossie wailed.

"But it will be fun to watch them knock the house down!" Freddie reminded her.

That afternoon when school had been dismissed a large crowd of boys and girls gathered on the driveway to watch the house wreckers.

While one group of workmen was busy getting the machinery ready, another group was tearing out woodwork which could be used again. There was a steady procession of men carrying out mantelpieces, fine old doors, and stair rails. These were piled into a truck and driven away.

Finally a man climbed into the cab of a huge machine from which a crane protruded. At the end of the crane was a giant iron ball.

"That's the wrecking ball!" Freddie called out in excitement. "Watch it smash the house!"

At that moment Mr. Tetlow came from the school building and stood beside the Bobbseys. A man stationed near the house gave a signal, and the huge ball swung against the old house.

Crash! The ball smashed into the roof and tore a big hole. Splinters of wood flew in all directions.

Then as the operator pulled the ball back for another swing, Nan Bobbsey screamed loudly:
"Stop!"

CHAPTER XVIII

THE TREASURE

THE wrecker looked from the cab of his machine. "Did someone call me?" he asked.

Nan, followed by Mr. Tetlow and the other Bobbseys, ran over to the huge machine. "Will you stop for a few minutes, please?" she pleaded. "I think I heard a cat crying."

"I heard it too!" Freddie agreed excitedly. "Do you think it could be Snoop?"

"There it is again!" Bert exclaimed. "It's coming from the kitchen!"

The children and the principal ran into the house and back to the kitchen. What a sight met their eyes! The logs in the fireplace had tumbled forward and scattered on the floor. The metal plate wall back of it had crashed inward and lay on top of the logs.

Nan dashed over to the opening. As she leaned forward to look in, something jumped onto her shoulder.

Snoop! Covered with soot!

Freddie grabbed his pet and hugged him. "I'm so glad we found you!" he cried. "Please don't go away again!"

Snoop snuggled up under Freddie's chin and purred happily.

"Where do you suppose he was?" Bert said, curious. He pulled out his flashlight, stepped into the fireplace, and gasped.

"That wall we saw was a fake!" he exclaimed.

"There's another one back of it with steps leading to the roof! Snoop must have climbed to the roof and then was afraid to come back."

"And went down the chimney steps!" Flossie cried. "She's a smart kitty."

"Oh, boy!" Freddie exclaimed. "A mystery stairway! You've really found something, Bert!"

"That terrific bang on the house by the wreckers did it," Bert replied.

"I wonder where the steps go?" Nan said. "Maybe to a secret room!"

"Let's go up and see!" Flossie proposed, starting forward.

Mr. Tetlow caught her by the hand. "Not so fast, young lady," he cautioned. "I think one of the older children should go first."

"I will," Nan volunteered. While Bert held the flashlight so that it shone in front of her, Nan crept up a few steps. Suddenly she called out, "There's a box here!"

"Ooh!" Flossie cried. "Can you bring it out?"

In reply Nan carefully backed down the steps, holding a black metal box in her hands. She put it on the floor and they all waited breathlessly while she fumbled with the clasp.

In another minute the box was open. Inside were two small chests—one a velvet jeweler's case and the other of carved wood with a slide top.

"Open them quick!" Freddie urged, his blue eyes snapping excitedly.

With shaking fingers Nan pressed a little catch on the velvet box. It popped open. Inside lay a pale green cameo carved with a woman's head. It was surrounded by a row of sparkling diamonds!

"How bee-yoo-ti-ful!" Flossie gasped, taking the brooch from its satin bed and holding it up to the light.

"It must be very valuable!" Mr. Tetlow exclaimed.

"Let's see the coins!" Bert urged. He picked up the carved box and slid off the cover. The interior was filled with square-shaped coins embossed with various figures.

"Ah! Obsidional coins!" Mr. Tetlow observed. "They're very rare."

The children bent over to examine the silver pieces. One was eight-sided and bore a design of a castle with three towers. Another had an inscription in the middle and a seal in each corner.

"These are really museum pieces!" the principal said, closing the box again.

"They must be Mrs. Marden's treasures," Nan said, her brown eyes shining.

"Let's take them to her right away!" Flossie urged.

"I'll drive you over," Mr. Tetlow offered, as excited as the twins.

When they left the old house, the principal told the wreckers they could continue their work. Then he led the Bobbseys to his car. In a short while they parked in front of the Rolling Acres Nursing Home.

Flossie jumped out and ran up the walk, calling, "Mrs. Marden! Mrs. Marden!"

Mrs. Marden came hurrying down the stairs as they entered. "What is it?" the elderly woman inquired anxiously. "Is something wrong?"

"We've found your treasure!" Freddie shouted.

"You mean my kitten?" Mrs. Marden asked, noticing the pet that Freddie still clutched in his arms.

"No, your missing presents!" Flossie cried, holding out the metal box.

Mrs. Marden sank into a chair. "You dear children!" she exclaimed. "Where did you find that box?"

Excitedly the twins told the story of the wrecker and hearing the cat cry and the discovery of the treasure in the old fireplace.

"Of course!" the woman cried. "Now I remember! That secret stairway was a favorite hiding place of mine. I knew no burglar would ever think of removing the metal wall I put up when I moved. But," she continued ruefully, "I forgot that was where I had hidden the box."

Freddie had been waiting to speak. Now he asked anxiously, "Is Snoop your cat?"

Mrs. Marden pulled the little boy over to her and put her arms around him. "We called him Midnight," she explained. "The secret stairs were his favorite place for a snooze. Often he would disappear and I would find him there. But now the stairway is going to be destroyed. Will you keep my pet for me?"

Freddie looked relieved and nodded eagerly. Then he asked, "But how did Mr. Ryan get him? He gave Snoop to me!"

"Mr. Ryan?" Mrs. Marden looked puzzled. Then she brightened. "That must be the nice man at the store. I remember now I always thought he looked kind, and when I wanted to find a good home for Midnight I asked him if he would take my cat. I'm glad he gave the kitten to you if you like him."

Freddie hugged Snoop. "We all love Snoop," he said earnestly. "He's a member of our family!"

"You children are wonderful detectives," Mrs. Marden said. "You found both my treasures and my cat!"

"Snoop found me first!" Freddie said. He told Mrs. Marden about his adventure in the store when he had met Mr. Ryan.

"Midnight is a very smart cat," she commented, and then thanked all the twins again for recovering the heirlooms.

Mr. Tetlow drove the children home. When they related the day's adventures to their mother and father, Mrs. Bobbsey remarked proudly, "I told Mrs. Marden you twins were good at solving mysteries!"

The next day the Bobbseys met Nellie and Charlie on the way to school. Nellie ran up to Nan.

"What happened yesterday?" she asked. "I saw you dash into the old house, and then later you all went off with Mr. Tetlow. Charlie and I are dying to hear about it!"

The twins quickly brought their friends up to date on the events of the day before. "Oh, Nan, that's simply super!" Nellie exclaimed. "Mrs. Marden must have been thrilled!"

"You're great detectives!" Charlie praised them. Then as the group approached the school he said under his breath, "Look what's waiting for us!"

Danny Rugg was standing on the steps. "I hear you found your old cat," he sneered as the Bobbseys came up. "Too bad you didn't look there sooner instead of going all the way to Maple Street!"

"So you did make that call!" Nan said indignantly.

"Sure!" Danny boasted. "I could have had you dumb kids running all over town if I'd wanted to!"

"They're not so dumb," Charlie spoke up. "I know someone who thought an old muff was a cat!"

Danny reddened and turned away. Bert called after him, "How did you get into the old house?"

The bully came back, a smug look on his face. "The house is gone now, and I can't have any more fun scaring you," he said, "so I guess I might as well tell."

"Did you have another key?" Freddie asked.

"No. I was in the yard the day you found that secret door in the cellar. When you left, I figured out a way to open it from the outside. So, after that, I had no trouble getting in whenever I wanted to!"

"You didn't scare us, so you were wasting your time," Bert replied.

"By the way," said Nan, "I wonder how Snoop got into the house."

This was a mystery none of them could solve. Perhaps it had been through a broken window. "Or he might have run in behind that janitor sometime," Bert suggested. "Then he was afraid to climb down through the window."

"He must have lived on mice," Flossie spoke up.

"When they started knocking down the house, he got scared and called to us!" Freddie guessed.

At this moment the bell rang, and the children went in to their classrooms. Instead of beginning the lessons, the teachers announced that there would be a special assembly.

The auditorium buzzed with questions as the children filed into their seats. They grew quiet when Mr. Tetlow walked to the front of the stage.

"I have an important announcement which I am very happy to make," he began. "I don't know whether all of you have heard of the exciting events of yesterday afternoon. Thanks to the efforts of the Bobbsey twins, some very valuable possessions of the former owner of the old house next door were found and returned to her."

He told the story of the missing heirlooms and the Bobbseys' search for them.

"Mrs. Marden is very thankful," he want on, "and as an expression of her gratitude, she has asked me to sell these valuable articles and wishes to donate the proceeds to help buy equipment for our new gymnasium."

As Mr. Tetlow spoke these last words there was a burst of applause and cheers from the audience. Then as the noise died down, a clear young voice was heard. It was Freddie Bobbsey's.

"But *we* didn't really find the treasure," he said. "Snoop, our cat, found it!"